"Laney, I want you to meet the town's new deputy sheriff, Nick Rogers."

His handshake was firm, his skin warm and dry. His dark-eyed gaze made the already hot day sizzle.

"You're new to the area?"

"I'm adjusting," he said, never taking his eyes off her. He had the kind of face that she'd thought only existed in the movies. Rugged and yet as handsome as any she'd ever seen with dark hair and blue eyes. But it was the way he stood, his head cocked to one side, an air of confidence about him that drew her like a moth to flame.

"You should come to my cousin's engagement party."

He smiled. "Thank you, but I really couldn't intrude."

"It's no intrusion," Laney said. "That's the way things are done around here. Haven't you seen the baby shower and anniversary notices in the local newspapers, inviting the whole county? Welcome to small-town America."

"A lot different from Houston," Nick said.

"Everyone will be there. Wear your dancing boots."

Nick met Laney's gaze. "Save me a dance?"

B.J. DANIELS

THE NEW DEPUTY IN TOWN

HARLEQUIN®

TORONTO • NEW YORK • LONDON
AMSTERDAM • PARIS • SYDNEY • HAMBURG
STOCKHOLM • ATHENS • TOKYO • MILAN • MADRID
PRAGUE • WARSAW • BUDAPEST • AUCKLAND

This book is dedicated to Chris and Jessica Kerr,
the cutest couple I know and the sweetest.
It's a joy to know the two of you.

ISBN-13: 978-0-373-69269-9
ISBN-10: 0-373-69269-2

THE NEW DEPUTY IN TOWN

ABOUT THE AUTHOR

Award-winning journalist turned author, B.J. had thirty-six short stories published before her first romantic suspense novel, *Odd Man Out,* came out in 1995. Her book *Premeditated Marriage* won *Romantic Times BOOKreviews* Best Intrigue award for 2002 and she received a Career Achievement Award for Romantic Suspense. B.J. lives in Montana with her husband, Parker, three springer spaniels, Zoey, Scout and Spot, and a temperamental tomcat named Jeff. She is a member of Kiss of Death, the Bozeman Writer's Group and Romance Writers of America. When she isn't writing, she snowboards in the winters and camps, water-skis and plays tennis in the summers. To contact her, write to P.O. Box 183, Bozeman, MT 59771 or look for her online at www.bjdaniels.com.

Books by B.J. Daniels

HARLEQUIN INTRIGUE
851—HIGH-CALIBER COWBOY*
857—SHOTGUN SURRENDER*
876—WHEN TWILIGHT COMES
897—CRIME SCENE AT CARDWELL RANCH**
915—SECRET WEAPON SPOUSE
936—UNDENIABLE PROOF
953—KEEPING CHRISTMAS**
969—BIG SKY STANDOFF**
996—SECRET OF DEADMAN'S COULEE†
1002—THE NEW DEPUTY IN TOWN†

*McCalls' Montana
**Montana Mystique
†Whitehorse, Montana

CAST OF CHARACTERS

Nick Rogers—The new deputy sheriff was anything but what he appeared to be.

Laney Cavanaugh—The last thing she'd expected to find in Whitehorse was the man of her dreams. Too bad he wasn't the man she thought he was.

Laci Cavanaugh—When she decided to throw an engagement party for her cousin Maddie, she wanted it to be a killer party. It was.

Arlene Evans—Her new Internet dating venture had the potential to be the straw that broke the camel's back.

Bo Evans—He was getting married...just as soon as he took care of some unfinished business.

Violet Evans—Her mother would do anything to marry her off. But what would Violet do to stop her?

Charlotte Evans—She was just your average teenage girl. Or was she?

Zak Keller—His life depended on finding the man who'd witnessed his crimes—and killing him.

Geraldine Shaw—No one knew much about her except that she liked macaroon cookies.

Sarah Cavanaugh—She'd thought being a Cavanaugh would bring her everything she ever wanted.

Maddie Cavanaugh—The bride-to-be's secret was killing her.

Chapter One

Her hand trembled as she opened the closet to find the baseball bat where she'd hidden it in the very back corner. After last time, she'd considered getting rid of the bat. Instead, she'd wiped off the splattering of blood as best she could and kept it.

She wasn't stupid. She watched *CSI* and all the other forensics television shows. She knew about blood splatters, about DNA, about trace evidence.

But she also knew it wouldn't be good to change anything. Ritual, she knew, was important. It should always be a Saturday night. She should always wear the same blue dress she'd worn the first time. She should always use the old baseball bat she'd found.

"I thought you were going out with friends?" called a voice from the living room. She could hear the TV. One of those reality shows was on. "It's getting kind of late though to be going now, isn't it?"

She bit down on her irritation. She was sick of being told what to do. Sick of other people's expectations for her. She put the bat on the bed and reached for her blue dress. There was one little blood spot along the hem that she'd had trouble getting out. She frowned, worried that even one spot might be enough to change things. To ruin the routine. To jinx her.

She worried at the spot for a moment. Maybe she shouldn't go into town tonight. But it was Saturday. There would be a band at one of the bars. There would be men who would get drunk and want to dance with her.

She thought of the smell of them, the feel of their sweaty hands on the blue dress, the sound of their breathing as they pressed themselves against her.

She put on the dress and picked up the bat. A woman on TV was gagging loudly as if unable to swallow something revolting.

She went out the back door, letting it slam. It was Saturday night. She was wearing her blue dress. She had the bat. And wouldn't some man be surprised tonight.

Chapter Two

Sunday morning Laney Cavanaugh looked down at the book in her lap, then out at the country. She was having trouble keeping her mind on what was being touted *the* summer beach-book read. Maybe it required a beach.

This part of northeastern Montana couldn't be farther from the shore. She could see from horizon to horizon, the rolling landscape awash with tall golden grass that undulated in the morning breeze. Etched against the horizon to the east was the dark outline of an old windmill. To the southwest was the faint smudge of the Little Rockies and the Bear Paw Mountains. In between was prairie, miles and miles of it.

"Boring, huh?" her sister said as she came out of the house, the screen door slamming behind her. "No wonder Mother hated it here." Laci plopped down in the chair next to Laney's with a huge sigh.

Laney didn't hate it here. Coming here had

always given her a sense of peace. She liked the quiet, the only sound crickets chirping in the grass or the closer buzz of a bee in the flower bed along the porch. At night sometimes the wind blew or rain fell in a monotonous drone that lulled her to sleep.

Today though, she felt restless. The July air seemed to be holding its breath, waiting for something. She felt that same sense of anticipation inside her like the flutter of butterfly wings. Something was about to happen.

She didn't share these thoughts with Laci, who would have made fun of her. "You are *so* dramatic," her younger sister often said. "You should have been an actor or a writer or well, anything but an accountant."

"I'm going to bake some cookies," Laci said, shoving herself out of the chair. Her sister had never been able to sit still for long. It was only nine in the morning. Laci had already made them both breakfast including a blueberry coffee cake, a spinach-and-bacon quiche and smoothies. But then Laci wasn't happy unless she was cooking.

"I've never understood why Gramps keeps this place," Laci said as the screen slammed behind her.

Laney understood. This house was all they had left of their daughter Geneva. She and Laci had been born here. That was before their father had been killed in a car accident between here and the small Montana town of Whitehorse to the north.

The first settlement of Whitehorse had been nearer the Missouri River. But when the railroad came through, the town migrated five miles north, taking the name with it.

The original settlement of Whitehorse was now little more than a ghost town except for a handful of ranches and a few of the original remaining buildings. It was locally referred to as Old Town.

Old Town Whitehorse had once been the home of horse thieves who'd been either hanged or forced out by the early settlers. Laney's family had been one of the first to settle here, just miles from where the Missouri River wound a deep cut through the land.

This house and the early memories of their daughter were all Gramps and Gramma Pearl had. Titus kept the place up as if he believed that one day Geneva would return.

Laney and Laci visited each summer for the promised two weeks. Laney felt guilty that it wasn't more, but both she and Laci had their own lives, Laci in Seattle and Laney in Mesa, Arizona. The house sat empty the rest of the time. Waiting for someone who was never going to return.

Laney tried to go back to her book, but her mind kept wandering. She found herself looking down the long dirt road. If anyone had been coming, she would have been able to see the dust cloud miles away.

Nothing moved. Huge cumulus clouds bobbed along in an ocean of blue as the sun rose higher and the day began to get hot. A cloud floated over, casting a dark, cool shadow over her. Laney shivered, sensing a change in the air.

An instant later she was startled by the unexpected thunder of hooves as her cousin Maddie came riding around the end of the house. Maddie leaped off her horse in a cloud of dust, her face flushed with excitement under her western straw hat.

"I heard you were here," Maddie said as she bounded over the railing just as she'd done since she was a child. "Mother's coming by later, but I couldn't wait so I rode over," she said as she gave Laney a hug.

"Got in last night." Laney smiled in spite of herself as she looked at her cousin. Now nineteen, Maddie hadn't changed that much from the gangly freckle-faced girl she'd been. She was tall and slim to the point of being skinny, with a mop of thick reddish-blond hair and light blue eyes. She wore a western shirt, jeans and boots.

"Where's Laci?" Maddie asked excitedly. "Cooking, I'll bet. Oh, what is that heavenly smell?"

From inside the house came the warm rich scent of chocolate-chip cookies baking even though it was way too hot to bake. As if that had ever stopped Laci.

"Who wants a warm cookie?" her sister called on cue from inside the house.

"Guess who!" Maddie called back laughing, then looked at Laney, her expression sobering. "I wish you lived here. I hate these short visits. They are never enough." She gave Laney another hug, hanging on longer this time.

Laney sensed a small shudder in her cousin's thin frame. She pulled back, taking Maddie's arms to look at her, and felt her flinch. Shoving back Maddie's shirtsleeve, Laney saw dark bruises, each spread evenly apart as if someone had grasped her too roughly.

"What is this?" What she wanted to say was "who did this to you?"

"You know me," Maddie replied quickly, drawing her sleeve down over the bruises. "I've always been such a klutz. It's nothing."

It was something; Laney could feel it as Maddie flashed her a reassuring smile that didn't quite ring true and hurried into the kitchen.

THE NEW DEPUTY SHERIFF, Nick Rogers, had been covering the weekend shifts until Sheriff Carter Jackson returned from Florida. So he wasn't surprised when he got called out on another assault Sunday morning.

There'd been two assaults since he'd taken the job. The victims were men who'd been attacked outside one of the bars on a Saturday night when the place was packed and there was a live band. Which probably explained why no one heard a disturbance in the parking lot.

He found Curtis McAlheney at the bar nursing a beer. Nick slid up onto the stool next to him and ordered a cup of coffee since it was only nine-thirty in the morning.

Curtis had a split lip, a black eye, a broken nose and was stooped over as if his ribs were bothering him.

"Broken or cracked?" Nick asked.

"Cracked, but they hurt like hell," Curtis said.

"You see your assailant?"

Curtis looked over at him. Thirty-something, he had thinning brown hair that stuck out the bottom of his John Deere cap. His eyes were small and brown, and his belly hung over his jeans into a T-shirt that proclaimed he was God's gift to women.

"Assailant?" Curtis repeated. "Didn't see no *assailant*—just some bastard with a baseball bat."

"You see his face?"

Curtis shook his head regretfully. "It was dark. He hit me from behind, knocked me down then beat me up good. He was big, I can tell you that much."

Nick nodded. This was pretty much the same description he'd gotten from the other men. Nick suspected the assailant was anything but big. A big man armed with a baseball bat would have done a lot more damage. "He rob you?"

Curtis looked sheepish. "I imagine he planned to. I think he came to his senses and took off before I got up and took that bat away from him and showed him what for."

Right. The motive in all the cases didn't appear to be robbery since nothing was taken but each man's pride. The assailant had just attacked, beaten up the men and taken off.

"Before you left the bar, did you get into a disagreement with anyone?"

"Naw. I just had a few beers, danced a little."

Same story Nick was getting from the others, although he suspected each had had more than a few beers.

"Well, if you think of anything else," Nick said finishing his coffee.

"Has to be some bastard not from around here, ain't that right, Shirley?" Curtis said to the bartender.

The bartender, a fifty-something stick of a woman, nodded. "No one around here would do something like that for no good reason."

Nick suspected whoever the assailant was, he had a reason, one good enough for him anyway. Tossing money on the bar for his coffee and a tip, Nick left as his cell phone began to vibrate.

"Trouble down in Old Town Whitehorse," the dispatcher said. "Alice Miller says someone stole her chickens."

AS MADDIE RODE OFF, LACI PUT her feet up on the porch railing and sighed. "We need to have a party for her."

Laney looked up from her book although she hadn't been reading. She'd been thinking about her cousin.

Laci took a cookie from the plate she'd brought out earlier. They'd had cookies and lemonade on the porch and talked about old times, although Laney hadn't been able to shake her worry for her cousin.

"An engagement party," Laci said between bites.

"I'm not sure that's a good idea," Laney said. "Didn't Maddie seem…different to you?"

Her sister shot her a look. "She's lost a bunch of weight since last summer. Don't all soon-to-be brides do that though?"

Maybe. "She's too skinny, but that's not what I'm talking about. She doesn't seem…"

"Happy?" Laci started laughing. "Maddie could be the poster child for happy."

"I felt like she was trying a little too hard," Laney said. She'd seen her cousin when they'd gotten into town last night. Only Maddie hadn't seen them. Laney had called to her cousin who was leaving the back way just as they were coming in the front. But their cousin obviously hadn't heard them over the din of the bar as she left. "Like last night when we saw her leaving the bar. She wasn't with her fiancé."

Her sister groaned. "Maddie's fine. I'm sure she wasn't doing anything more than dancing with a few ranch hands just like we were. She left the bar alone, didn't she?"

Laney nodded.

"See. Maddie's just stretching her wings a little."

Maybe, but Laney wasn't convinced.

"Now help me with the engagement-party menu," Laci said excitedly. "I want it to be something the town of Whitehorse has never seen. What do you think we should have to eat?"

"Don't you think you should at least talk to

Maddie about this first? Maybe she doesn't want an engagement party."

Laci laughed as she rose from her chair. "Who doesn't want an engagement party? I'm going to start going through some of Gramma's old recipes. I think I'll do all desserts. What do you think?"

But she didn't wait to hear what Laney thought. The screen door slammed. Laney stared out at the horizon, trying to put her finger on what was bothering her about Maddie. Maybe it was the way her cousin had talked about her fiancé, Bo Evans, as if she would die without him. Or the way she played with her engagement ring. Or the way she brushed off her original plans to attend college, even giving up a scholarship.

All of that Laney could chalk up to love.

All except the bruises on Maddie's arm.

And Laney's own feeling that something wasn't right with her cousin.

She closed her book, glancing up the lane. That sense of nagging expectation washed over her again as if at any minute she would see someone coming down the road toward the house with bad news.

"Let's take some cookies to the hospital for the nurses," Laney said as she brought the plate and lemonade glasses into the kitchen to find her sister deep in an old cookbook. "I want to go visit Gramma."

Laci looked up. "Do you mind going without me? I hate seeing Gram like that and I really need to get to work on this party. I'm thinking it should be next

Saturday. I'm sure we can use the community center."

Laney knew how hard it was for her sister to see their grandmother Pearl after her stroke. Gramma's eyes were open, but she was unresponsive. It was questionable if she could even understand what they said to her. Or if she recognized her granddaughters at all.

Gramma Pearl had been in the hospital with pneumonia when she'd suddenly had a stroke. Gramps said she'd been upset about some things that had been going on in Old Town Whitehorse.

"I think we both should go see Gramma," Laney said. "As it is, Gramps won't be happy with us since we didn't attend his church service this morning at the center. Maybe we can bribe him with some of your cookies because you know he'll be with Gramma."

Laci nodded although with obvious reluctance. "As long as you keep him from talking about Mother. I can't bear it. He really believes Geneva will just come home one day as if nothing happened. Why can't he accept that she's gone and won't ever be back? For all we know she's dead."

"He has to believe he'll see her again," Laney said although she agreed with her sister. Wherever Geneva Cavanaugh Cherry was, this was the last place she'd ever return.

DEPUTY SHERIFF NICK ROGERS had never been to Old Town Whitehorse before. He would have missed it entirely, if he hadn't slowed down to let a dog cross in front of his patrol car and seen the sign barely sticking up out of the weeds beside the road.

Whitehorse. Population 50.

He truly doubted that, given the age of the sign.

Nick had driven five miles through rolling grassland and open sky. He'd heard this land called the Big Open. He could well understand why.

And after all that way, he'd arrived in Old Town Whitehorse. Well, what was left of the original Whitehorse. There were a few buildings. No store. No gas station. No bar. Just what appeared to be a community center, an ancient abandoned gas station and a few houses still standing.

He could make out the trees and roofs of a few farms or ranches not far from town, but this whole place felt more like a ghost town than anything else.

One big old house in particular reminded him of a haunted house he and his friends used to throw rocks at when he was a kid. He stared at the two-story house. It sat apart from the others. The paint had peeled and it appeared kids had broken out most of the upstairs windows. The lower ones were boarded up. The mailbox out front had fallen over, but he made out the word *Cherry* as he drove past.

He rolled his window down and breathed in the smell of fresh-cut hay. He couldn't help but laugh at himself. He'd been looking for a place to escape. Literally. And he'd found it in Montana. No one would ever look for him here—let alone find him. At least if he hoped to stay alive.

If Whitehorse wasn't the end of the earth, then Old Town definitely was. He'd heard someone joke the first night he'd gotten into town that "Whitehorse isn't the end of the earth, but you can see the fires of hell on a clear night."

Nick had been to hell. Maybe that was why he'd felt at home here right off.

Alice Miller lived in a big white ranch house west of town. As he pulled into the yard, two blue heelers with spooky white eyes came out to bite at his tires.

The house was sheltered by rows of trees that had to stand over fifteen feet tall. Past the house and trees, the country ran south through open prairie to what appeared to be a thin line of green. The Missouri Breaks.

He could understand why Old West outlaws had made this isolated, underpopulated country their hideouts. It had worked for Kid Curry and Butch Cassidy and the Sundance Kid. At least for a while.

Nick was counting on it working for him.

At least for a while.

He eyed the barking dogs. He had a healthy respect for ranch dogs since arriving in Montana and waited until an elderly woman in a housedress and apron opened the front door and called off the dogs before he got out.

Alice Miller was petite with serious blue eyes and bobbed gray hair. She led him around the back of the house to a chicken coop.

"There you are," she said as if that should clear things up for him.

He looked into the empty coop. Yep, things were clear as mud. "How many chickens did you have?"

"A dozen layers, four roosters and three old stewing hens."

"Nineteen chickens and they were all gone this morning," he said.

She nodded and waited as if she expected him to produce them like a magician pulling a rabbit out of his hat.

"That's a lot of chickens to disappear," he remarked. When he'd found this job, he'd been amazed at the kind of calls a deputy sheriff in White-horse, Montana, had to deal with. Dog at large, owner warned. Drunken disturbance at rodeo, citizen given ride home. Missing resident, found two doors down.

As a big-city cop, he'd dealt with every crime imaginable. At least he thought he had. But he'd never been called out to investigate nineteen missing chickens.

He was out of his league and he knew it.

"What do you think happened to them?" he asked Mrs. Miller.

She cocked her head and looked up at him as if he might be pulling her leg. "Clearly someone stole them."

"How do you know a coyote or something didn't come in and eat them all?"

"You see any feathers?"

Actually, he did. There were feathers all over the chicken coop.

"You see any blood, any bones?" she asked with growing impatience. "Where are you from anyway?"

"Houston."

"Where's your Texas accent?" she asked.

"I wasn't born there. My father was in the military. We traveled all over." It was the story he'd come up with. It made things simpler. And safer.

Mrs. Miller let out a little huff sound and put her hands on her hips. "Aren't you going to look for fingerprints? Tracks? Something?"

Fingerprints? She couldn't be serious. As for tracks, it had rained the night before. There were lots of tracks, all appearing to have been made by her dogs.

"I got wash to do," she said and headed for the side yard.

He circled the chicken coop, feeling like a fool. He'd never tracked anything in his life. This was nothing like chasing a convenience-store robber down an alley and over a couple of fences.

To his surprise, he found some tracks that looked out of place. He squatted down next to one of the prints. The sun had already baked the surface of the yard. The print was that of a boot. A small one. A kid's.

Nick walked around to where Mrs. Miller was hanging sheets and towels on a clothesline.

"Who all lives here?" he asked.

"Me and my husband. He's out cutting hay. Why?"

"You have any grandchildren, any children who have been over to visit in the last day or so?"

"No. What does that have to do with my chickens?"

"No neighbors with kids?" he asked.

Alice Miller wrinkled her brow. "There is that boy, his aunt and uncle are renting the farm next door."

Nick pulled out his notebook and pencil. "What do these chickens look like?" He glanced up when she didn't answer and saw her expression. "Okay, would you be able to recognize them if you saw them again?"

"Just find my chickens," she said and went back to hanging up her wash.

Nick followed the boy's tracks, wondering how the kid had pulled it off. Nineteen chickens were a lot. Wouldn't they have caused a ruckus that could be heard up at the house?

He could envision Mrs. Miller with a shotgun coming out in her flannel nightgown, blood in her eye. So why hadn't that happened?

He glanced up at the sound of a dog growling and realized he'd reached the farm closest to the Millers'.

"Hello!" he called and eyed the dog. It wasn't a blue heeler, but some kind of mutt, large and hairy. "Hello!" He feared the dog would key on the fear in his voice and attack. Easy, Cujo.

"The chickens aren't hurt," said a young voice from the back steps of the house. The kid was twelve tops, lanky with sandy-blond hair and big ears.

"That's good," Nick said. "Could you call off your dog?"

"Prince, no," the boy said. The dog eyed Nick for a moment, then ambled over to the kid and sat down.

"I'm Deputy Sheriff Nick Rogers." He'd taken the *Rogers* from an old western he'd seen on television the night he'd left town. "What's your name?"

"Chaz. It's actually Charles, but that's what everyone calls me," the boy said. "My aunt and uncle are in town if you're going to arrest me. I'm not sure when they'll be back."

"Where are Mrs. Miller's chickens?"

He pointed toward a shed at the back of the property. "I was going to return them. Really."

"Why'd you take them in the first place?" Nick asked, glancing toward the house. "You need the food?"

"No," Chaz said indignantly as they walked back to the shed. A ruckus was coming from inside. "I got plenty to eat and I didn't take anyone's chickens."

Right. That was why Nick had just followed the kid's boot prints to his house straight from the chicken coop.

At the shed, Chaz opened the door a crack so Nick could see that all nineteen chickens were there. The chickens looked a little funny to him, their feathers kind of glued to them, but what did he know about chickens other than buying cut-up fryers in plastic wrap at the grocery?

"We need to get the chickens back to Mrs. Miller," Nick said.

"I know. I was thinking about how to get them to her," the boy said.

"Why not take them back the same way you stole them?"

"I told you, I didn't steal them."

"Right."

Just then one of the chickens made a beeline for the door, slipping through to take off at a run across the yard.

Before Nick could react, Prince darted after the chicken. "No!" Nick called to the dog. Too late. In an instant, Prince had the chicken clutched in his jaws and was prancing back toward them looking like the cat that ate the canary.

To Nick's astonishment, the dog dropped the slobber-coated bird at Chaz's feet, the chicken jerking to its feet unhurt. The boy grabbed the bird and tossed it back in the shed.

"See the problem?" Chaz said. "I took one back when Prince brought it home. I didn't know he was going back last night to get them all."

Nick stared at the dog. "Are you trying to tell me that Prince stole the chickens?"

Chaz nodded. "I told him not to, but Prince likes to collect things." The boy shrugged. "It's his only bad habit. Other than that, he's a really good dog."

Prince was leaning against the boy's leg, looking up at him. Chaz patted the dog's big head. The dog's tongue lolled. He could have been smiling.

Nick swore, pulled off his hat and raked a hand through his hair. "I've got to tell you. I don't know much about transporting chickens. I'd consider any idea you might have on how to get them back in Mrs. Miller's chicken coop."

"I've been thinking on it," Chaz said. "I might have an idea."

TWO HOURS LATER, ALL NINETEEN chickens were safely back in Mrs. Miller's chicken coop. Nick left Chaz on the Millers' porch eating fresh-baked apple pie and sipping a large glass of milk, Prince at his feet. Chaz had promised to keep a closer eye on his dog.

Nick was feeling good. He'd solved his first mystery in Montana. With a little help from a kid and a dog.

Back at his office, he was hoping the rest of his shift would be as uneventful when he looked up and saw a young reddish-blond woman get out of her car. As she started toward his office, another car raced up, tires screeching as the driver came to a stop and rolled down his window.

The woman turned. Clearly, the two knew each other. Nick watched from his window, not liking the change in the woman's demeanor when she saw the young man behind the wheel. Nick had covered enough domestic-violence cases to recognize one on the street.

The woman said something to the man, who appeared to be about her age, no more than twenty, then she turned and started walking toward the sheriff's department again.

The man threw open his door and went after her, grabbing her arm and swinging her around to face him.

Nick shot out of his chair, hitting the door at a run. As he exited the courthouse building, he heard the raised voices.

"Let go of her," Nick said in his calm cop voice.

"This isn't any of your business," the young man said. He had brown hair, brown eyes, classic good looks.

"Let go of her," Nick repeated.

The young man did, but with obvious reluctance and definitely an attitude. "I'm not breaking any law."

"Domestic abuse is against the law," Nick said.

"Domestic abuse?" The young man scoffed at that. "My girlfri—fiancée and I were just having a little private disagreement."

The young woman was rubbing her arm where the man had grabbed her. "He's right. It's nothing."

"Why don't you step inside and we can talk about it," Nick said to the woman.

She shook her head, eyes wide. "It's nothing, really."

"You were headed for my office. There must be something you wanted."

"I wasn't. That is, I was going up to the treasury

department upstairs. I got turned around." She was lying and Nick could see that she was afraid.

"What's your name?" he asked the young man.

"Bo Evans." He said it as if it should mean something. It didn't to Nick.

"You live around here?"

"Old Town Whitehorse." Bo was giving him an are-you-stupid look. "You're not from around here, huh?"

"What's your name?" Nick asked the woman.

She hesitated. "Maddie Cavanaugh."

She was edging toward her car. "I have to get to work," she said.

"Where do you work?" Nick asked.

Maddie Cavanaugh looked around as if searching for an answer. "In Old Town Whitehorse. I just help Geraldine Shaw out."

Nick nodded and turned to Bo Evans. "Disagreements are one thing, but you were scaring your fiancée. Keep your hands off her when you're angry, okay?"

Bo Evans shook his head as if in disbelief. "I wouldn't hurt Maddie. I love her. We're getting married. What is wrong with you, man?"

Nick watched them leave in separate cars, worried about the young woman. Whatever she'd been planning to tell someone at the sheriff's office, her fiancé had done a good job of changing her mind.

Chapter Three

Laney Cavanaugh saw him as she came out of the hospital. He stood across the street talking to her grandfather Titus.

She wasn't sure what it was about the man that caught her attention let alone held it as she crossed the street. He wore jeans and boots, a tan short-sleeved shirt and a cowboy hat. Nothing unusual about that in Whitehorse, Montana.

He had one boot sole resting on the bumper of Titus's pickup truck and was leaning forward, listening intently. She tried to imagine what her grandfather might be saying that would require that kind of attention as she crossed the street.

It wasn't until she was almost to the pair that the sun glinted off the man's silver star and she realized that the tan shirt was actually part of a uniform.

"Laney, I want you to meet the town's new deputy sheriff, Nick Rogers," Titus said. "This is my granddaughter Laney Cavanaugh."

She smiled and extended her hand, which quickly disappeared into the lawman's large sun-browned one. His handshake was firm, his skin warm and dry. His dark-eyed gaze made the already hot day sizzle. She sensed that odd expectation in the air that she'd felt earlier as if she wasn't the only one holding her breath.

"I was just telling Nick that you and your sister are staying out at my daughter's place," Titus said. "Nick's new to the area. I'm sure it's all a bit strange after Houston."

"I'm adjusting," he said, never taking his eyes off Laney. He had the kind of face that she'd thought only existed in the movies. Rugged and yet as handsome as any she'd ever seen, with dark hair and eyes. But it was the way he stood, his head cocked to one side, an air of confidence about him, that drew her like a moth to a flame.

"I told Nick we'd have to get him back down our way for dinner sometime," Titus said.

"He should come to the party," Laci said, coming up behind them. She'd hung back to give their grandmother's nurses the chocolate-chip cookies. Laney could feel her sister's gaze on her, hear the humor in her voice. "Shouldn't he, Laney?"

"Of course," Laney said because what else could she say under the circumstances? She looked down, surprised to see he was still holding her hand.

"What kind of party is this?" he asked as he let go, as if as reluctant to break the connection as she'd been. His gaze, however, came right back to her after he shook her sister's hand.

"It's our cousin's engagement party," Laci said.

He smiled. "Thank you, but I really couldn't intrude."

"It's no intrusion," Laci said, grinning curiously from Laney to Nick. "The entire town is invited and half the county. That's the way things are done around here. Haven't you seen the baby shower and anniversary notices in the local newspaper inviting the whole county? Welcome to small-town America."

"A lot different from the big city," Nick said. "But still I don't think I—"

"It's for our cousin Maddie Cavanaugh and her fiancé Bo Evans," Laci interrupted. "It would be a good time to meet more of the locals. Everyone will be there."

Laney saw the change in Nick's expression. "Maybe I *will* reconsider," he said. "When is this party?"

"Saturday afternoon," Laci said. "Wear your dancing boots. Gramps will be playing his fiddle as part of the Whitehorse Country Band."

Nick met Laney's gaze. "Save me a dance?"

She nodded, feeling sixteen again and just as foolish because she was beginning to think this engagement party for Maddie wasn't such a bad idea after all.

ARLENE EVANS LOOKED ACROSS the table at her handsome son and smiled. She'd suggested dinner at the Hi-Line Café because she had something important to announce.

"I'm going to have the steak sandwich," Bo said, closing his menu. He glanced toward the street and drummed his fingers on the table as if bored.

Arlene tamped down her annoyance. "Have whatever you want," she said, feeling magnanimous. Bo was the light of her life. *Her son.* The one who would carry on the family name. It was especially important to have a son when you lived on a farm. Sons stayed and worked the place and, although Bo had shown little interest in farming, she knew he would once he was married.

Daughters on the other hand, well, they were supposed to get married and leave.

She let her gaze shift from her son to her youngest daughter, Charlotte. Charlotte was staring at a lank of her long straight blond hair, looking for split ends. Arlene applauded Charlotte's interest in her looks at seventeen. At least one of her daughters understood the importance of looking her best from her hair to her prettily painted acrylic nails.

Arlene glanced at her other daughter and scowled. Violet, her *unmarried* daughter, was her burden to bear. Not pretty, not overly bright, certainly not ambitious, Violet was thirty-four with few prospects. No matter what Violet wore, she looked...well, frumpy.

Her hair was a dull brown and her complexion muddy, and her nails! Arlene had done everything possible to break Violet of biting her nails and it had done no good.

Arlene feared her daughter would never marry and leave home as was natural. And how would that reflect on Arlene? She couldn't bear such a blight on her as a mother.

"I'll have a cheeseburger with fries and a chocolate milk shake," Violet said tentatively.

"Are you sure you don't want a nice salad, dear? All that fried food. It isn't a problem for the rest of us, but with you watching your weight…"

Violet closed her menu. "Why don't you order for me, Mother?"

Arlene thought she detected an edge to her daughter's voice, but that would be so unlike Violet that she dismissed it.

"So what's this about?" Bo asked impatiently. "You said you had something you wanted to tell us?"

Arlene refused to be rushed. Fortunately, the waitress came to take their orders just then. A steak sandwich and jojos for Bo, the grilled chicken salad for Violet, a side salad with vinegar and oil for Charlotte and a strawberry milk shake, the fish basket with fries for Arlene.

"So did anything interesting happen last night?" she asked Violet after the waitress had gone.

Violet looked at her brother. "Well," she said dragging out the word, "I did see Maddie at the bar last night. She was dancing with *Curtis McAlheney.*"

"So?" Bo snapped. "It's not like we're married yet. She can dance with anyone she wants."

"Curtis McAlheney?" Violet let out that irritating loud laugh of hers. "He's old enough to be her father!"

"Please! Could we just have one meal together without you two arguing?" Arlene glared at Violet, took a breath and let it out slowly, upset to hear about Maddie.

She wondered if Maddie had been drinking. She wouldn't have been surprised, given that Charlotte had gotten served when the bars were really busy even though she was only seventeen. Or maybe the girls had fake IDs. That would be just like Maddie.

"You weren't with Maddie, Bo?" Arlene asked, surprised and a little concerned. She'd thought that he was meeting Maddie when he'd left the house before his sisters last night.

"I went to Havre with some friends," he said, obviously not happy to hear that Maddie had been at the bar—and dancing with Curtis McAlheney even though Curtis was no prize. "It's not like Maddie and I are attached at the hip, you know."

"You're right," Arlene quickly agreed. "It's good to have friends and do things with them even after you're married."

"*If* he gets married," Violet said under her breath.

"What is that supposed to mean?" both Arlene and Bo demanded. Charlotte hummed quietly to herself, apparently oblivious to the rest of them.

Violet only gave her brother one of her that's-for-me-to-know-and-you-to-find-out looks.

Arlene wanted to slap her. Instead, she decided it was time to make her announcement. "I have great news. I've started a home business."

Both Bo and Violet were noticeably surprised. Charlotte glanced up, but went back to her split ends; she would never need a dating service.

"What kind of business?" Violet asked as if worried she might have to work it.

"On the Internet," Arlene said excitedly. She'd done her best to find Violet a man, throwing her together with every eligible man she could find in several counties. Now it was time to expand her territory. "It's an Internet dating service for rural singles."

Violet gasped.

Bo began to laugh, shaking his head as his gaze went to Violet then his mother. "This is going to be good."

ON SATURDAY, NICK TOLD HIMSELF he had no business going to a party in Old Town Whitehorse or anywhere else. His plan had been to keep a low profile while in Montana. That meant doing his job, staying to himself, having as little contact with the locals as was necessary.

It wasn't as if it had slipped his mind why he was here or what was at stake if he screwed up. He had to keep his head down. Dancing with a pretty young local woman with emerald-green eyes wasn't just risky business. It could get him killed.

And yet, dancing with Laney Cavanaugh was all he could think about as he checked his messages at his office before getting ready to head to Old Town.

He told himself he was just doing his job by going to the party. That he wouldn't have accepted the party invitation if it hadn't been for Maddie Cavanaugh's and Bo Evans's engagement. He hadn't been able to forget the fear he'd seen in Maddie's eyes that day outside his office. Nor could he shake the instant dislike he'd felt for Bo Evans. The kid was trouble. Nick had seen enough young men like Bo to spot his kind a mile away.

And what would just one dance hurt?

Nick looked up at the sound of a man clearing his throat.

"I—I—I was attacked."

The man standing in his doorway was average height, average build, average in most every way. He looked vaguely familiar.

"I'm the reporter for the *Milk River Examiner.* I tried to do a story on you when you came to town," the man said as if seeing Nick attempting to place him.

"Right."

"Glen Whitaker," the man said. He'd looked sheepish when Nick had first looked up, but now he appeared a little aggravated at not being remembered. Or maybe it was because Nick had declined to be interviewed.

"You say you were attacked?" Nick asked. The man didn't appear to be in pain. Nor did his clothing suggest an attack. He wore dark slacks, a white shirt, loafers. He obviously was a transplant from somewhere else. His hair was slicked back in an old-fashioned cut although he appeared to be in his thirties. Hard to tell age with a man like that.

"The attack happened a month ago, right before you were hired," Glen Whitaker said, glancing around as if he wanted to make sure no one was listening. There wasn't anyone in the office and the dispatcher's desk was far enough away she couldn't have heard. Nor did she seem even interested in what the reporter was doing here.

"Sit down," Nick said as Glen drew up a chair, pulling it close to the deputy's desk. "You say it happened before I was hired. Did you report it?"

"No." Glen looked nervous. "I wasn't sure."

"You weren't sure you were attacked?" Nick was beginning to wonder about this guy.

"You see, I was told that I'd been down at Old Town. It's a near ghost town south of here by the Missouri Breaks."

Nick nodded. "I've been there."

"Anyway, about a month ago I woke up beside the road, my car smashed into a fence post, miles from everything. I couldn't remember anything. I later found out that I was in Old Town Whitehorse. I had two large bumps on my head that I thought must have caused the memory loss."

"Were you drinking?" Nick had to ask.

"I don't drink. Several people saw me leave the Whitehorse Community Center and can attest to the fact that I hadn't had a thing to drink. That was the night before. I woke up beside the road the next morning feeling like I'd been run over." Glen leaned in closer. "When I got home I found bruises all over my body as if I'd been beaten."

Nick had been thinking the man was a nutcase. But his story was a little too much like the others Nick had been hearing. Also, the attack had been on a Saturday night.

"Would you say the bruises indicated you might have been kicked? Or beaten with a weapon of some sort?" Nick asked.

Glen Whitaker sat back, relief drowning his features. "You believe me then?"

"There have been some other reports of this sort of thing."

"I was afraid to come in." Glen looked away as if too upset to go on. "I was afraid you'd think I was crazy."

Nick pulled out a report. "When exactly did this happen?"

Glen stood abruptly. "I don't want to file a complaint."

"Why not?"

"I don't want this all over town. That's why I

came to you. You don't know anyone. I just needed to tell someone."

"But don't you want your attack on record?"

The reporter wagged his head. "And have it end up in the newspaper? No way." He started backing toward the door.

"Okay," Nick said putting the form away. "I won't make out a report. But tell me when it happened. There appears to be a series of these attacks. Yours might have been the first."

"Saturday, four weeks ago, when that Bailey woman went missing. I can't remember the exact date."

Nick had heard about the Bailey woman, that she'd been discovered down in the Breaks and everything that had happened because of it.

"You have any idea who's responsible for these attacks?" Glen asked.

"Not yet, but your information might prove critical to the investigation." Nick checked his calendar. "From what I can tell, yours was the first attack."

"No kidding." Clearly, he was glad he wasn't the only one. "I'm afraid I wouldn't be much help. I still can't remember anything about those lost twenty-four hours." He paused. "There was one thing though." He looked sheepish again. "It's probably nothing."

Nick smiled to himself. He'd been a cop long enough to know that whenever anyone said "it's probably nothing," it was usually something.

"I smelled something on my clothes afterwards," he said, flushing a little. "I think it might have been perfume."

Nick could see how uncomfortable this admission made the reporter. "Do you have a woman friend?"

Glen shook his head. "I like women, don't get me wrong."

"Of course. But you can't recall being around a woman that day."

"I can't recall anything, that's the problem."

"Okay, this perfume. You recognize the scent?"

Another shake of his head.

"What was it like?"

"Some flower I think."

That narrowed it down. "A flower you'd recall if you smelled it again?"

"It was an old flower, you know the kind—" he hesitated "—that older women wear."

Nick nodded. "Okay, that could help." He couldn't imagine how, since Glen Whitaker had no idea who he'd come in contact with before he'd woken up beside a road in the middle of nowhere. Apparently an older woman.

"Okay," Glen echoed. "I just thought you ought to know."

"I'm glad you came in," Nick said.

Glen hesitated at the door. "My editor still wants a story on you."

"Thanks," Nick said, "but I'll pass. I'm shy and the story of my life would put your readers to sleep."

Glen shook his head. "We print stories like that all the time."

"Yeah," Nick agreed with a laugh, "I've read your paper."

As Glen left looking like a whipped puppy, Nick checked. Sure enough, there'd been an assault every Saturday night for apparently the last four weeks.

But this Saturday everyone would be in Old Town Whitehorse at Maddie Cavanaugh's engagement party. At least this afternoon.

As he stood to leave for the party, Nick thought of Maddie. That young woman was in some kind of trouble. But he didn't know what to do about it if she wasn't willing to tell him.

He considered confiding in Maddie's cousin Laney, telling her his concerns, and quickly nixed the idea. He didn't know Laney Cavanaugh, although he felt as if he did. Crazy.

Still he couldn't shake the thought of inviting her to town for dinner one night and seeing what he could find out about the cousin and her fiancé. Maybe he'd ask Laney at the party. Maybe while they were dancing.

Just a man doing his job.

As he started to leave his office, he glanced back at his desk. Time for a reality check, he thought as he walked back and unlocked the bottom drawer of his desk. The cell phone he'd bought when he'd left California was right where he'd put it. He only turned it on to check for messages once a day.

He hadn't checked it yet today. Hell, he'd forgotten for a while there what he was doing in Montana. He picked up the phone and turned it on. No messages.

Nick breathed a sigh of relief although he knew it was just a matter of time before he got the call. One that would tell him it was time to return to California. Or a call that would tell him his cover was blown and to run.

He turned off the cell phone and put it back in the bottom drawer, locked the drawer and stood for a moment, hesitating. Just checking the phone had been a reminder how foolish it would be for him to get too involved, either in his work or with anyone while in Montana.

That was why he should just back off. If Maddie Cavanaugh really was in trouble, then let her come to him. And as for Laney Cavanaugh... He shook his head, reminding himself that his life here was one big fat lie. The closer he got to Laney Cavanaugh, the greater his chance of being found out. And if that happened, he was as good as dead.

DURING THE WEEK, news of the engagement party for Maddie Cavanaugh and Bo Evans spread like wildfire through the county. Few people were apt to turn down a party, especially one being thrown by a Cavanaugh. Some just wanted to come to critique Laci Cavanaugh's cuisine. There was a rumor going round that she was planning to start her own catering business and was trying out recipes at the party.

Only two of the people who heard about the party were upset.

Arlene Evans was insulted that she hadn't been asked to at least bring some of the food for the party. After all, she had taken the most blue ribbons at the Phillips County Fair and the Whitehorse Fourth of July picnic.

And in case no one had noticed, Bo was her son.

"The mother of the groom isn't allowed to throw the engagement party," Alice Miller told her one afternoon at the Whitehorse Sewing Circle. "Actually, you shouldn't even be allowed to work on your daughter-in-law's wedding quilt, but since we're shorthanded with Lila Bailey and Pearl Cavanaugh gone…"

That had distracted Arlene. "I still can't believe that Lila Bailey would just up and run off like she did." She waited a moment for the other women in the circle to jump in. Arlene lowered her voice. "I always wondered about the paternity of her oldest daughter, Eve. She didn't look anything like the rest of them."

"Arlene," Geraldine Shaw said impatiently and totally out of character. Pearl was the one who usually chastised Arlene for talking about anything interesting. "You missed a stitch. Perhaps you should tend to your quilting."

Geraldine's rebuff was so unexpected that Arlene was at a loss for words.

DOWN THE ROAD FROM WHITEHORSE, Maddie Cavanaugh took the news of the engagement party even
harder.

"No, that's not possible. Laci can't, I mean, she
didn't say anything about—"

"It's wonderful that your cousin is doing this for
you," her mother said, cutting her off. "You should
be thankful."

Since Sarah Cavanaugh had married into the family, she'd been trying to gain her rightful place.
While she lived in a nice enough house to the east
of Old Town Whitehorse, she had always been over-
shadowed by Titus and Pearl Cavanaugh, who were
like royalty in this part of the county.

Sarah had felt slighted even though she'd tried to
be part of this community and the Cavanaugh family.
This party for her daughter though would finally put
her part of the family in the limelight. It was only
right that she and Maddie would get some attention.
It angered her that Maddie didn't want the party—
and she said as much to her.

"It just seems…premature," Maddie said.

"Premature? You've been engaged for over a
month."

"Bo and I haven't even set a date."

"Well, then I suggest you do. You can announce
it at the party," Sarah said.

"I wish Laci had asked me about this," Maddie
said. "Saturday? I had plans that night."

"The party's in the afternoon. But even if it runs into evening, you can just change your plans," Sarah said gruffly, frowning at her daughter who had once been so malleable.

Sarah blamed it on the fact that Maddie had been spending way too much time away from her fiancé. Sarah had hoped Bo would be able to handle Maddie. But she'd heard her daughter had been seen at the bars, dancing with older men. If she hadn't known how much Maddie loved Bo and needed him, Sarah Cavanaugh would have been worried.

Chapter Four

All week, Laci had been baking, forcing anyone who came by to try her treats. From candy to cookies to tarts and turnovers, and individual cobblers and cheesecakes, she'd worked to come up with the perfect dessert menu with growing expectation of Saturday's event.

Laney had her own expectations as the day finally arrived. She hadn't seen Deputy Nick Rogers, wasn't even sure he would show for the party, but she was still anxious anyway—and upset with herself for being so excited about seeing him again. She'd seen the man only once, had barely said two words to him. This was so unlike her to be excited about a man she'd just met. Unlike her younger sister, she *always* looked before she leaped. But this time, she just wanted to jump—and that should have scared her.

Maddie had stopped by the day after Laci had started inviting everyone to the engagement party.

"I wish you'd mentioned a party to me," Maddie had said. "Not that I don't love the idea."

Laney had seen that Maddie was anything but delighted with the party idea.

"Don't thank me," Laci had said, giving her cousin a hug. "I just wanted to do something special for you. Because you're special."

Maddie's blue eyes had filled with tears. She'd bit her lip and said nothing more.

But Laney had seen her expression. Maddie wasn't just displeased about the party, she seemed... worried. Since that day, Maddie hadn't been by, which was strange in itself.

When Laney had called to make sure she was all right, Maddie had told her she'd taken a job helping Geraldine Shaw clean out her attic.

"I like this kind of work. I think it might be like accounting," her cousin had said. "Something that actually makes sense, you know?"

"Maddie, is anything wrong?" Laney had asked. "Because if you need someone to talk to—"

"Wrong? Of course not. Everything is wonderful. I'm marrying Bo." Laney had heard the catch in her cousin's voice. "I can't imagine life without him."

"You don't have to," Laney had said.

"No, I don't. Bo is perfect for me." Another catch in her voice.

"Still, every bride-to-be gets cold feet," Laney said.

"Not me." She'd hesitated. "We've had our problems, just like any other couple. But once we're married things will be different."

Her cousin didn't really believe that marriage solved the problems, did she? "Maddie—"

"I'm fine. Really. There is nothing to worry about."

But Laney had worried.

Now she heard a car and glanced at her watch. Aunt Sarah had called and offered to take some of the desserts for the party to the community center in her van.

Sarah had also helped with the decorations and volunteered to taste treats as was needed over the week.

"Because of your darned sister, I've gained ten pounds," Sarah said as she came into the house.

"I had to refuse to taste another thing," Laney said. "Laci was giving me a toothache. Is Maddie ready for the party?"

Sarah nodded, her face beaming. "This is so exciting. A party for my baby. Thank you for doing this. I can't tell you what it means to us."

"It's all Laci's doing," Laney said, but she could see what it meant to Sarah. She wasn't so sure about Maddie. She considered broaching her concerns about Maddie to her aunt but Laci came out of the kitchen with a container full of bite-size chocolate-covered cherry cheesecakes, and Sarah began oohing and aahing over them. They *were* beautiful. And much too pretty to eat.

After Sarah left with the back of her van full, Laney checked her watch again.

"Shouldn't we be getting over to the community center?" she asked her sister.

Laci was nervously staring through the oven glass. "Just a few more minutes on the caramel puffs. They're best if served warm. I have the macaroons resting at room temperature."

Laney shook her head. "Lace, there is no way we're going to be able to eat all of this."

A knock at the door surprised them both. Laney thought it might be Sarah back for something. "I'll get it. You watch your puffs."

Geraldine Shaw was standing on the porch. She wasn't dressed for the party. She looked harried and upset as Laney opened the door.

"Where's Maddie?" Geraldine asked abruptly.

"I don't know."

"She was gone when I returned from the post office and my mother's diamond bracelet is missing," Geraldine said, looking past Laney. "Are you sure she isn't here?"

"Yes. She might be at home or at the community center, but I'm sure if the bracelet is missing, Maddie had nothing to do with it."

"I showed her the bracelet when we were cleaning out some things. When I left, I told her to be sure and put it back in the box." Geraldine sounded near tears. "It's *gone*."

"I'm sure it's just misplaced," Laney said with concern. "Why don't I call Maddie and see if—"

But Geraldine was already off the porch steps,

huffing as she climbed into her car and tore off in a cloud of dust.

A shriek came from the kitchen. Laney went racing in to find her sister hysterical.

"My caramel puffs fell. This is an omen. The party is going to be a disaster."

Laney calmed down her sister and sent her to get ready. She didn't have the heart to tell Laci that there were worse problems with the party than some fallen caramel puffs. Not that Laci would appreciate the gravity of the missing bracelet. Not when gravity had ruined her caramel puffs.

WHEN NICK DROVE into Old Town Whitehorse, he was amazed at how many vehicles were parked around the community center. Laci Cavanaugh was right about one thing: the entire county had turned out for the engagement party.

He parked and walked down the road to the center, reminding himself he was on a case—even if not technically on duty. He planned to leave in time to watch the bars tonight in Whitehorse. It was Saturday and if the assailant was true to form, he'd be attacking some poor cowboy before the night was over.

As Nick slipped into the crowded building, the band broke into a country ballad. His best friend would have gotten a real kick out of this.

Just the thought of Danny O'Shay cut like a blade into his heart. Danny couldn't see this because Danny was dead. And Nick was the reason.

"Deputy Nick Rogers," said a female voice dripping with sugar. "I don't think we've met."

A tall, thin middle-aged woman with a braying laugh reached for his hand and shook it vigorously. "I'm Arlene Evans. This party is for my son and his fiancée."

Bo's mother. While her son was a nice-looking young man, Arlene Evans was one of those raw-boned ranch women.

"And this is my daughter, Violet," Arlene said as she grabbed the woman's arm next to her and literally dragged her over. "Violet, say hello to Deputy Rogers."

Violet Evans gave a meek nod.

"Hello, it's nice to meet you," Nick said. With Violet it was hard to tell her age. She was as plain as any woman he'd ever seen. She had her mother's raw-boned look but on a larger frame.

"Deputy Sheriff Rogers is new in town and single," Arlene said and winked at Nick. "The Whitehorse grapevine."

Violet stared at the floor, but Nick noticed a flush creep up her neck and several veins pop up prominently. The woman was more than embarrassed.

"If you'll excuse me, I need to speak with Titus," Nick said as the band took a break. As he escaped, he heard Arlene chastising her daughter about not saying something interesting to make Nick stay. This was the woman who'd raised Bo Evans, he reminded himself. It could explain a lot.

"I see you made it," Titus said and looked past him to the crowd. Titus Cavanaugh was a large, white-headed man with a powerful voice and a strong handshake. "My granddaughters are here somewhere. Quite the turnout. I hope you've tried some of Laci's desserts. She really did go all out, but then that's Laci. She was born with a spoon in her hand." He laughed at his small joke.

Nick wanted to ask about Laci and Laney's parents. He hadn't heard anything about them. But he didn't get the chance.

Across the room, he spotted Maddie Cavanaugh. She was dressed in a pale blue dress the same color as her eyes. Even from here he could see that her face was drawn, her freckles seeming to jump out. She looked upset.

He saw that she was listening to something Arlene Evans, her future mother-in-law, was saying. Arlene had a firm grip on Maddie's arm and seemed to be trying to lead her out the back door.

"Here's one of my granddaughters!" Titus announced.

Nick turned to come face-to-face with Laney Cavanaugh. She was dressed in a peach-colored dress that fell like water over her curves. Her face had a glow to it that had nothing to do with makeup, and those eyes, those amazing emerald eyes...

Past Laney, he saw Arlene Evans drag Maddie outside.

Nick cursed under his breath. "Excuse me a minute. I'll be right back," he said to Laney and made his way through the crowd after Arlene and Maddie.

WELL, THAT WENT WELL. Laney tried to hide her disappointment. She'd been looking forward to seeing Nick Rogers all week. In fact, when she'd spotted him talking to her grandfather, she'd made her way through the crowd, too impatient to wait for him to find her.

Or maybe worried he wouldn't.

Laney wasn't used to behaving like this. She turned away, fighting the urge to flee. Instead, she went over to the dessert table to see if she could help her sister.

"It's a success," Laci announced and sighed. "My first catered party. I can tell you now. I'm opening my own catering business, Cavanaugh Catering, right here."

"Here?" Laney stared at her sister. Not because this surprised her. The way Laci loved to cook, it was the perfect career choice. "Here in Old Town?"

"Not just Old Town and Whitehorse, silly. I was thinking that it's crazy that nobody lives in Mother's house. I could run my catering business from the house. That way I would be close to Gramma and Gramps. But I would cater the whole county."

Laney didn't know what to say. Laci had always been the one who couldn't wait to get out of here after their two-week summer visit each year. "What about Seattle?"

"It will always be there," Laci said with a laugh.

Laney eyed her sister. "This seems kind of sudden."

"Not really. I've given it a lot of thought. I've already told Gramma."

Gramma hadn't been responding to anything since her stroke.

"It was the weirdest thing," Laci confided. "She looked right at me. I swear she squeezed my hand. It was like there was something she wanted to tell me, needed to tell me, then she closed her eyes…"

"She's happy for you," Laney said quickly, not knowing if that was true or not. Gramma Pearl had always encouraged them to do what made them happy. Laney wasn't sure what their grandmother would think about Laci staying here though. But she was positive what Gramps would say. Titus would be thrilled.

"I thought I'd tell Gramps after the party," Laci said. "Oh no, we're almost out of those chocolate-covered cherry cheesecakes. I should have made more."

Or kept Violet Evans away from them, Laney thought as she watched Violet devour the last of the little cakes and then move down the buffet table toward the macaroons, stuffing a handful into the big pockets of her jumper when she thought no one was looking.

But Laney was distracted by the sight of Geraldine

Shaw heading for the dessert table. Had she found her diamond bracelet? Laney could only hope so. She glanced around for Maddie, but didn't see her anywhere.

BY THE TIME NICK STEPPED OUT through the back door of the community center, whatever Arlene had dragged Maddie out there for was over.

The two were standing a short ways from the back door. Maddie had her arms folded over her chest, her eyes on the ground. She'd been crying. Arlene was standing over her, glowering down at her.

"Is there a problem?" Nick asked pointedly.

Arlene turned in surprise, her expression instantly changing as she stepped back from Maddie. "Why, Deputy, you're missing the dance. My daughter Violet—"

"I was hoping to dance with the bride-to-be," Nick said looking at Maddie. He could hear the music coming from the center, but he was more interested in what Arlene had been saying to Maddie. Whatever it had been, he was betting it hadn't been good. Arlene had been giving Maddie hell—and at her engagement party. That didn't bode well for their future relationship.

Arlene's look soured as she glanced from Nick to Maddie and back.

"I wanted to wish her well on her engagement," he added. "If you'll give us a moment," he said pointedly to Arlene.

"Of course," the older woman said, sending a warning glance at Maddie before she went back inside.

"Are you all right?" he asked.

Maddie looked up, her blue eyes filled with tears. She made a swipe at them. "I'm fine."

"I don't think so."

"Please," Maddie said looking nervously toward the door. "Don't. You'll only make things worse."

"Is that possible?" he asked.

Maddie dried her eyes.

"Let me help you," Nick said.

"What's going on out here?" asked a strident male voice.

Nick recognized it without turning. Bo Evans. His mother's doing no doubt. She'd sent him out here. "I meant what I said," Nick whispered to Maddie. "I can help if you'll let me."

She gave him an indecipherable nod and, putting a smile on her face, stepped around him.

Nick watched as Bo pulled Maddie to him none too gently and the two disappeared back inside. Nick swore and went to find Laney Cavanaugh.

But as he entered the center, he heard a bloodcurdling scream and saw the crowd converge to a spot in front of the dessert table.

Nick pushed his way through to find Geraldine Shaw on the floor. She was gasping for breath, her face bright red, her eyes bulging. "Everyone get back!" he yelled as he knelt down next to her. "Can you hear me?" He could see the panic in her face.

She tried to lift her arm from the floor and he saw what was left of a macaroon clutched in her fist.

Nick felt the woman's panic. He'd been here before. But like before, there was no time to do anything. The poison was too fast acting. Geraldine Shaw went into convulsions and he caught the familiar odor of bitter almond just before she died.

Chapter Five

"Internal asphyxia," the state coroner said as he came out of the autopsy room. "She literally died due to lack of oxygen."

"And the macaroon she had in her hand?" Nick asked.

"Laced with enough cyanide to kill a horse. But her age and health were obviously factors in how quickly the poison acted."

Nick cursed under his breath. He'd known Geraldine Shaw was poisoned with cyanide. He'd just hoped he was wrong. "What about the other macaroons?"

The coroner shook his head. "We also checked the other desserts that you brought us. None had poison in them."

"So it was just the one cookie?"

"Apparently so."

Nick shook his head. How could the killer be sure that the one poisoned cookie went to the right victim? Or was it random? He raked a hand through his hair, worried that this had nothing to do with Geraldine Shaw and a whole hell of a lot to do with him.

But there was no way Keller could have found him because no one knew he was here, right? Nick hadn't trusted anyone after what had happened in L.A. It was just a coincidence that Geraldine Shaw had been poisoned with cyanide—the same poison that had been used to kill his friend Danny.

Cyanide was a common poison and yet he still wondered if his cover was blown. If this was Keller's way of letting him know that he'd found him.

Nick felt that old panic rise in him. He couldn't bear the idea of being responsible for another innocent person's life.

He'd leave town. He could be gone from this place in a matter of minutes. He'd traveled light getting here. He could travel even lighter leaving.

He tamped down his fear. Keller was desperate. He was through playing games. He would just kill Nick and get it over with. Why kill some poor woman instead? It made no sense.

Nick tried to relax. With the sheriff in Florida, Nick was tempted to call in a state investigator to help with the case, but he feared that would only attract more attention to the case—and him, something he couldn't do.

Busy with the murder Saturday afternoon, Nick hadn't done surveillance at the bars as he'd planned and there'd been another attack. Same MO as the others. The assailant had used a baseball bat.

"Do you know who baked the cookies?" the coroner asked.

Nick nodded. Laci Cavanaugh. He thought of her sister Laney. Hell, he hadn't even gotten to dance with her. Which, all things considered, was probably a blessing in disguise. He couldn't let it slip his mind that Keller would be frantically looking for him. Nick's days here were numbered. As soon as he got the call, he'd be gone as quickly as he'd appeared in Montana.

"Unfortunately, the cookie was smashed in Geraldine Shaw's hand so we have no way of knowing how the cyanide got into the cookie."

Which meant anyone at the party could have doctored the macaroon.

Nick thanked the coroner and headed for Old Town Whitehorse and the Cavanaughs.

"POISONED?" LANEY CAVANAUGH couldn't believe what she was hearing. She'd been sitting on the porch when she'd seen dust in the distance. Her first reaction to seeing the patrol car coming up the road had been a flutter of excitement. Her heart had kicked up a beat at just the sight of Nick as he'd climbed out.

She stood now, going to stand at the porch railing, looking out at the country, but seeing nothing through her fear. "I thought Geraldine had a heart attack?"

"I'm going to need to talk to your sister," he said, joining her at the railing.

"You don't really believe that Laci poisoned that woman!" she said, trying to keep the tremor out of her voice.

"Frankly, all I know is that Geraldine Shaw was poisoned by a macaroon that your sister baked."

"What was her motive?" Laney demanded, turning to look at him.

"You tell me."

Laney was reminded of Geraldine's visit just before the party. "We barely know Geraldine Shaw." Unfortunately though, Geraldine had accused their cousin of taking her diamond bracelet. Not that it had anything to do with this.

She saw him glance to where Laci's car was usually parked, the space empty.

"Laci went into town."

"When will she be back?"

"I'm not sure. I hope you're looking into other suspects."

"Such as?" he asked. He had the darkest eyes.

Laney shook her head. She didn't have a clue who might have a grudge against poor Geraldine Shaw, let alone who would want to kill her. She shuddered at even the thought of one of Laci's cookies containing *poison*.

"Where were you when Geraldine Shaw collapsed?"

She thought for a moment. "I had gone over to see if Laci needed any help."

"So you were behind the tables or in front of them?"

"I was standing at the end."

"And what was Laci doing?"

Laney tried to picture it in her mind. "She was re-filling the dishes with the desserts and fretting because she wished she'd made more of some things than others."

"Such as?"

"The bite-size chocolate-covered cherry cheese-cakes and—" She stopped and looked at him. "The macaroons. There was only one left on the plate. Earlier I'd seen Violet Evans stuffing her face and her pockets. Laci was about to refill the plate when someone picked it up."

"You don't remember who?"

She shook her head. "Violet was standing there with her mother. I saw Charlotte join them. Laci was reaching for the plate to refill it when someone took the last macaroon."

"Geraldine Shaw," he said. "Did you hear anyone offer her the cookie?"

Laney shook her head. "The band had started up again and everyone was talking."

"So the poisoned macaroon could have been meant for someone farther down the table even past Arlene. You remember who was standing next to her?"

"Sorry."

He nodded. "Please have your sister give me a call when she gets back." The deputy sheriff put his hat back on, then hesitated. "I'm sorry we didn't get that dance," he said, then gave her a quick nod and left before she could say, "Me, too."

Laney watched his vehicle disappear down the dirt road, dust billowing up behind it, before she hurried into the house to get her car keys.

ARLENE EVANS WAS FURIOUS. It was so like Geraldine Shaw to have a heart attack at Bo's engagement party of all places. If the woman wasn't feeling well she should have excused herself. Geraldine had spoiled everything in more ways than one.

To make matters worse, Arlene's Rural Montana Meet-a-Mate Internet dating service wasn't taking off. Everyone she'd talked to didn't want their photo and personal information out there for just anyone to see.

"I can't believe this," she muttered as she stared at her computer. Nothing was going right. Bo and Maddie had gotten into a fight right after the ambulance had pulled away with Geraldine—and Bo had taken off angry.

Not that Arlene could blame him. She just wanted to know if they were broken up for good. She always thought Bo could do better. Case in point: This morning Violet had announced she'd seen Maddie at the bar again last night dancing with anyone and everyone. Surely there was a better match for Bo.

Arlene glanced at her camera sitting next to her computer. She'd gotten some good shots of the guests before Geraldine had taken her swan dive under the dessert table. As she hooked the digital camera up to the computer and started going through the photographs looking for a possible match for her son, she got an idea.

She knew everyone in the county, knew more personal things about them than anyone else. And now she had photographs of a lot of the rural singles. They were just shy about her new business. Once they started getting called for dates, they'd thank her.

Arlene began to scan in the photographs, getting more excited as she went. She'd get money from the suitors. She wouldn't make as much this way, but she had to get her business going, and she had to find Violet a husband and Bo a better woman to marry.

She scanned in the photo of Violet at the party. Why had her daughter worn that horrible jumper? It just made her look bigger and fatter. Oh well, at least she'd changed before she'd gone into town last night with her sister.

Arlene cropped the photo and put it up, adding as glowing information as she could about her oldest daughter.

Then she flipped through the other candid photos she'd taken and stopped on one in particular. Deputy Sheriff Nick Rogers. She didn't know a lot about him, but she could always wing it.

She put his photo up on the dating site. Like the others, he'd thank her when she found him the woman of his dreams.

MADDIE CAVANAUGH STILL LIVED with her parents in a farmhouse outside of Old Town Whitehorse. Nick found it at the end of a dusty road in the middle of nowhere.

He noticed as he pulled into the yard that Maddie's car, the one he'd seen her driving the day she'd stopped by the sheriff's department, wasn't parked in the yard.

No one seemed to be home today. He started to turn around when the screen door opened. The woman in the doorway was fifty-something, blond and blue-eyed.

He climbed out of his patrol car and walked toward the porch. The sun beat down, baking the earth beneath his feet. "I'm Deputy Sheriff Nick Rogers. I was looking for Maddie Cavanaugh."

"Maddie? I'm sorry but she's not here." The woman introduced herself as Maddie's mother, Sarah Cavanaugh.

"Do you know where she is?" he asked, still worried about her. The murder of Geraldine Shaw had sidetracked him. But if anything, he was more concerned about Maddie Cavanaugh after that little scene he'd witnessed between her and Arlene Evans, her future mother-in-law.

"She stayed with a friend in Whitehorse last night. Wasn't that just dreadful about Geraldine collapsing like that? No one knew she had a bad heart. Why, she wasn't that much older than me."

He didn't tell her that Geraldine's heart had been

fine before she'd been poisoned. "Can you give me the name of this friend Maddie stayed with?"

"Why, you know I didn't even ask. She has lots of friends and stays at different places when she goes into town," Sarah said frowning. "Why do you need to see my daughter?"

"I'm questioning anyone who was close to Geraldine," he said.

"Oh. Well, I wouldn't say Maddie was close to her. I mean, Maddie helped her out from time to time. Geraldine paid her some measly amount. Geraldine was tightfisted and not close to anyone in Old Town. She stayed to herself mostly. I think she quilted with the women from the Whitehorse Sewing Circle…."

"You don't?"

"Me?" She seemed surprised by the question. "My mother did and her mother before her, but I found it all rather boring. I had too much to do raising my daughter and taking care of my home to spend a bunch of time sitting around with old women talking about the weather. My aunt Pearl, well, that's another story."

Nick could see that the house behind him was immaculate. He imagined Sarah Cavanaugh spent her days keeping it that way.

"Well, I appreciate your time. I'll try to catch Maddie later," he said.

"All right." There was a vagueness about Sarah Cavanaugh, like someone who'd spent too much time alone. He wondered what other farm and ranch women did during the day. Like Arlene Evans.

LANEY DROVE OVER to Geraldine Shaw's house. When she'd called Maddie earlier, her cousin had said that was where she was headed.

The women of the community always gathered to do whatever was needed in a time of crisis. Had her grandmother been able, she would have been at Geraldine's as well. Geraldine's husband Ollie had been dead for a little less than a year now. The widow had lived alone and as far as Laney knew, had no living relatives. There would be animals to feed, a refrigerator to be cleaned out, watering to be done. And a will to be read.

Maddie's car was parked in the yard along with a variety of other rigs. As Laney let herself in, she saw Maddie sitting in a corner, the rest of the local women scattered around the room.

At the center stood a man in a dark suit. He looked uncomfortable in a room filled with women. His suit and demeanor alone made him stand out in Old Town Whitehorse as either an insurance salesman or a lawyer.

Laney sat down next to her cousin. Maddie took her hand and squeezed it, eyes welling in gratitude.

"As Mrs. Shaw's attorney, I can tell you that before her death she made provisions for the disposal of her possessions as well as her house and property," the man said.

Laney looked down at Maddie's hand gripping hers. There were new bruises on her cousin's wrist. Laney winced at the sight of them. She was glad at least that Maddie wasn't wearing the missing diamond bracelet. She hadn't had a chance to speak to her cousin about Geraldine's visit yesterday. In the chaos after Geraldine's collapse, Maddie had disappeared and now certainly wasn't the time to try to talk to her.

"Since Mrs. Shaw had no living relatives," the attorney continued, "she has left her house and property to the Whitehorse Sewing Circle to be used as they see fit."

There was a murmur of surprise among the women.

"That is very generous," Alice Miller said to the nods of the other women.

The attorney cleared his throat. "As for her personal belongings, some jewelry and what money Mrs. Shaw had accumulated, those are to go to a Ms. Madeline Renée Cavanaugh."

Maddie burst into tears.

AS NICK WAS LEAVING Sarah Cavanaugh's house in the country, he got a call from one of the deputies that the man who'd been attacked behind the bar last night in Whitehorse had come in finally to file a report.

Someone had found Harvey T. Brown out behind the bar and called the sheriff's department. Brown, a known bar brawler who hated to ever lose a fight, hadn't wanted to make a statement because of his embarrassment at being beaten.

"Take Mr. Brown's statement and tell him I'll get back to him later," Nick told the dispatcher. He was starting to see a disturbing pattern. All of the attacks had been on a Saturday night. All except one behind a crowded Whitehorse bar. The oddball one was reporter Glen Whitaker's, but then Glen said he couldn't remember the attack. If his was part of the pattern, then it would have been the first. Glen, Nick recalled, had been the only one to mention perfume.

"Ask Mr. Brown if he remembered anything, like a sound or a smell," Nick said.

"Also, Laci Cavanaugh called. She said she'll be at home if you need to reach her."

HE FOUND LACI IN THE KITCHEN. Laney wasn't anywhere in sight and her rental car was gone. He should have been relieved. It had been difficult earlier keeping his visit professional when what he'd really wanted to do was invite her to dinner.

"Can we talk while I cook?" Laci asked, visibly nervous. "I do better when I cook."

"What are you making?" he asked as he watched her drop a stick of butter into a skillet on the stove and begin to chop cloves of garlic.

"Shrimp scampi. I would love to bake something for dessert, but after what happened—"

"Your sister told you that Geraldine Shaw was poisoned."

She nodded. "I can't believe it."

"How well did you know Geraldine?"

"I didn't. I mean I've seen her around. My grandmother knew her because she was part of the Whitehorse Sewing Circle. I don't think I've ever said two words to the woman."

"What about your grandmother? Did she get along with Geraldine?"

Laci laughed as she swept the chopped garlic into the melted butter, the scent wafting through the kitchen and making his stomach growl. "Gramma gets along with everyone. She's one of those people who never has a bad word to say about anyone." Laci rolled her eyes. "I'm serious. She hates gossip and won't even allow Arlene Evans to talk about other people when she's around."

Laci stopped, her eyes tearing up. "You know my grandmother had a stroke and is in the hospital."

"I'm sorry. Can you think of anyone who had a motive for killing Mrs. Shaw?"

She shook her head.

"So tell me where you were when Geraldine Shaw collapsed."

Laci said she'd been behind the serving table setting out the desserts. "The desserts were going fast. I was worried I hadn't made enough."

"The macaroons?" he asked.

"When I looked there was only one left on the plate." She shook her head as if surprised by that. "I reached for the empty plate to refill it when I heard someone gasping. When I looked up, Geraldine was on the floor and people were screaming."

"Why did you make macaroons?"

Laci frowned. "They're Bo Evans's favorite."

"Who told you that?"

"His mother. Or maybe it was his sister Charlotte.

Or was it Violet?" Laci shrugged. "It could have even been Maddie. I really can't remember. But you have to believe I would never put anything bad in what I cooked. What would that do to my catering business?"

He smiled to himself at her logic, hating to point out that if she put the poison in the macaroons, she wouldn't have to worry about her catering business. She'd be working in the prison cafeteria wearing a hairnet and making macaroni-and-cheese rather than shrimp scampi.

Laci turned to him suddenly, her eyes wide with alarm. "What is *this* going to do to my catering business? I mean I haven't really started it, but when someone drops dead from one of my macaroons at the first party I cater…"

She turned back to the stove, slid several dozen fresh deveined shrimp into the skillet with the butter and garlic, then began to chop some scallions with a cleaver, seeming to lose herself in her cooking again.

He watched her, fascinated. He could see that she loved cooking and believed her that she would never use her food to kill anyone.

"Tell me about the macaroons," he said.

"They're an old family recipe," she said. "My mother used to make them when Laney and I were little. It's the only thing I remember her making for us."

He heard the sadness in her voice. "Is your mother…?"

"Dead?" She shrugged. "One day we woke up and she was just gone. No one has seen her since." She slid the chopped scallions into the skillet, turned off the burner and looked at her watch.

"Expecting someone for lunch?" he asked.

"My sister and cousin. They should be here any minute." She must have heard his stomach growl. "You're joining us, aren't you? I always make extra."

LANEY DIDN'T GET A CHANCE to talk to Maddie until everyone left Geraldine's house.

"Geraldine was poisoned?" Maddie cried. "That's not possible."

Laney tried to calm her cousin. "Maddie, talk to me. I know something is going on with you."

Maddie was shaking her head from side to side and crying hysterically.

"Geraldine stopped by the house looking for you before the party. She was very upset. She thought you might know where her diamond bracelet was."

Maddie's tears slowed into jerky sobs. She looked up, fear in her eyes.

"Where is Geraldine's bracelet, Maddie?" Laney asked, her heart in her throat.

"I don't know. I put it back in the box before I left for the party. I swear I did."

Laney felt sick. "Who else might have come into the house after you left?"

"How should I know?" Maddie cried. "You know no one here locks their doors. Anyone could have stopped by and seen the jewelry box. I left it on the table with the rest of the things Geraldine had brought out for me to get ready."

"Ready for what?"

"To sell. Geraldine was going to sell some of the jewelry to a woman at an antique store in Billings."

"She was selling her jewelry?" Laney asked, her heart pounding. "Did she say why?"

Maddie shook her head.

Laney looked around the empty house, disgusted with herself for what she was about to do. But now both her sister and her cousin were in trouble. "Do you know where Geraldine kept her important papers?"

NICK HELPED WITH THE SALAD while Laci whipped up her favorite salad dressing. He couldn't help the excitement he felt at the thought of seeing Laney again. He tried to put his finger on what it was about Laney Cavanaugh and smiled to himself.

She made him think of a summer breeze billowing white curtains, fresh-baked apple pie cooling on a kitchen windowsill, hot dogs roasting over a grill in the backyard on the Fourth of July. It made no sense and yet it felt as if it were the only thing that made any sense in his crazy world.

He'd grown up in L.A., a rough street kid who'd straightened up in time to become a cop like the rest of his family. His old man had been a cop. So had three of his uncles and a couple of his cousins.

His father was Irish, his mother Italian. A terrible combination since they were both pigheaded and opinionated. His father was large and loud. Nick never thought he'd miss them, but he did.

He thought about Laney and how she wouldn't be intimidated by any of them, not his great-aunt Elvira or even his uncle Cosmos. Cosmos would love Montana. Nick doubted he'd ever been out of California since he'd migrated from New York back in the forties.

Nick heard a car, then another one, pull up outside. He warned himself not to do anything stupid as he watched Laci taste the salad dressing, closing her eyes, savoring it before announcing it was ready.

"You really do love to cook, don't you?" he said.

Her face softened. "It's all I've ever wanted to do. All my favorite memories are tied to cooking, the smells, the tastes, the feel of something as simple as stirring." She grinned. "You think I'm nuts, huh?"

"No, I like to cook. My Italian grandmother taught me to make a mean rigatoni."

"So you're Italian?" Laney Cavanaugh said from the doorway. "That explains your dark looks, but not the name Rogers."

He felt his pulse take off at just the sight of her. She was wearing white capri pants and a pale yellow sleeveless top, her skin tanned and sleek. Her blond hair was pulled back in a ponytail, her eyes that wonderful deep sea-green.

"I have no idea where the Rogers came from," he

said, feeling tongue-tied. For a moment talking to Laci, he'd forgotten his cover story and had offered more than he'd meant to.

Laney was eyeing him as if she'd seen that moment when he'd let down his guard. "Are you through grilling my sister?" she asked coming into the room.

"A little cooking humor?" Laci asked with a nervous laugh. "I told him I wouldn't poison anyone with anything I cooked and he believes me."

Laney lifted a brow. "Is that true?" she asked him pointedly.

"I've just begun my investigation. I'll let you know if I survive lunch."

NICK SMILED, REVEALING two small dimples Laney hadn't noticed before. She was so distracted that it took her a moment to register what he was saying.

"You're staying for lunch?"

"Your sister invited me and after watching her cook, I just couldn't say no."

She was going to have to sit through an entire meal with him? The last thing she wanted was the deputy sheriff at the table and she had a feeling her cousin didn't either as Maddie came into the room, stopping short at the sight of Nick.

"The deputy is joining us for lunch," Laney said to Maddie and stepped around the breakfast counter to join her sister at the stove.

"How you are doing, Maddie?" she heard Nick ask her cousin, but didn't hear Maddie's reply.

"What were you thinking, asking him to lunch?" Laney demanded in a hushed whisper to her sister.

"It was the polite thing to do," Laci whispered back. "Anyway, he's cute and you like him. I thought you'd be happy."

Laney groaned. She wanted to remind her sister that Nick was investigating a murder. But Laci being Laci knew she was innocent so wasn't in the least concerned.

Laney wished she shared her confidence in the judicial system. Unfortunately, Laney had seen enough true-life crime stories to know that innocent people went to prison all the time for crimes they didn't commit.

And after what she'd discovered in Geraldine Shaw's financial records, she was even more worried. Geraldine had been withdrawing rather large amounts of cash for months.

Given how frugally the woman had lived otherwise, the withdrawals sent up a red flag that it didn't take an accountant to question.

When Deputy Sheriff Nick Rogers found out about the unexplained monthly withdrawals, Laney knew he was going to think the same thing she did.

Someone had been blackmailing Geraldine Shaw—and the money had been about to run out.

Chapter Six

Nick could feel the tension at the table all during lunch. Maddie picked at her food, seeming to make a point of not looking in his direction. Her eyes were red from crying and he noticed that her hand holding her fork was shaking.

He had to wonder what had her so upset. He planned to ask her the moment he got her alone.

"This is an amazing meal," he said to Laci. "I can't remember one I've enjoyed more. What is the herb in the salad dressing? I can't quite place it."

She grinned, obviously pleased. "Chervil. It's the secret ingredient. You weren't kidding, you really do like to cook."

"I wouldn't lie about a thing like that."

"But you would other things?" Laney asked.

He glanced over at her. She hadn't said two words during lunch. Until now. "It's a figure of speech."

"Really?" she said sarcastically. Like a mother hen with Laci and Maddie, she was obviously angry with him for suspecting her sister and cousin. He found that and her all the more appealing.

Laci chattered about everything under the sun as they finished their meals, none of it requiring a comment from her sister or cousin. He concentrated on his meal, reminding himself why he was in Montana and just what he had to lose if he messed up. Getting involved with Laney would be the worst thing he could do.

"So do you like to cook, Laney?" he asked when Laci went into the kitchen to get the fresh fruit she'd prepared for dessert.

Laney's head jerked up as if she'd been miles away. "I can't even boil water."

"Now who's lying," Laci said as she returned with the fruit. "You have to excuse my sister. She's the *analytical* one." She grinned at Laney.

He looked from Laci to Laney, sensing an inside joke.

"I'm an accountant," Laney said with a sigh. "My sister has always given me a hard time because I look before I leap."

"What about you, Maddie?" Nick asked.

Maddie's eyes widened in alarm. "What about me?"

"Do you like to cook?"

She flushed and looked around as if trying to find a safe place to land. "Arlene is trying to teach me. She says I'm impossible."

"I'll teach you," Laci jumped in. "It's easy and fun. You'll see."

Nick doubted anything would be easy and fun with Arlene.

Maddie went back to moving her food around her plate.

He had to get Maddie alone to talk to her. Getting her to confide in him he feared would be much harder.

"I need to ask you a few questions," Nick said to Maddie after lunch. He saw the young woman glance at Laney. "It's just preliminary questions."

"I suppose it would be all right," Maddie said.

He gave her a reassuring smile. "Why don't we step outside to my patrol car."

Maddie hesitated, then followed him out. Once inside, he started the engine and saw her jump.

"Just turning on the air-conditioning," he said. "I want you to be comfortable." She was anything but. The slightest movement from him and she looked as if she might fly off the seat.

"Why don't you tell me about your relationship with Mrs. Shaw," he said.

"I didn't have a relationship with her."

"You worked for her. You knew her. Were you friends? Or just employee-employer?"

"The last. I just helped her out once in a while. I barely knew her."

Nick raised a brow. "I talked to her attorney this morning. I understand she left you everything but her house and property. It's not a lot but you're the only single person named in her will."

Maddie looked shocked that he knew this. "How did you..."

"You must have meant something to her for her to leave you all her personal possessions and what money she had."

"I don't know why she did that," Maddie said, sounding near tears. "I had no idea."

Nick believed that she hadn't been expecting the inheritance. He just couldn't figure out why Geraldine Shaw had put Maddie Cavanaugh in her will. But he suspected Maddie did know why and that was what had her so upset.

LANEY STOOD AT THE WINDOW, peering out through the curtains, worry making her ill.

"What is wrong with you?" Laci demanded as she dragged Laney away from the window.

"I probably shouldn't have let him talk to Maddie without an attorney present."

"For heaven's sake, why? It's not like she poisoned Geraldine," Laci said.

"I didn't tell you this, but Geraldine stopped by before the party. She was very upset. She couldn't find a diamond bracelet that she'd shown Maddie earlier."

Laci was shaking her head. "Maddie didn't take it."

"I hope not. What makes it more complicated is that Geraldine named Maddie in the will, leaving her all her personal belongings, including her jewelry."

"Well, see, then it doesn't matter. Maddie would get the bracelet anyway."

Laney stared at her little sister. Oh, to be Laci and live life in rose-colored glasses. "If the deputy finds out about the missing diamond bracelet, he might consider that a motive for murdering Geraldine. You know, to keep it from coming out that she'd taken the bracelet. After all, Maddie didn't know Geraldine was leaving her anything." At least Laney hoped Maddie's reaction at the Shaw house had been an indication of that rather than guilt. "And when you consider how oddly Maddie has been acting lately…"

"There's an explanation for all of this," Laci said looking worried. "I'm going to have to bake something. Chocolate. Chocolate pudding cake." She headed for the kitchen. "Maybe the deputy would like some."

Laney could only shake her head as she heard her sister searching for the recipe. She stepped back to the window as Maddie climbed out of the deputy's patrol car. Her cousin looked scared to death.

Laney's two-week summer vacation in Montana was up in a few days but she knew she couldn't leave until she'd cleared her sister—and cousin.

As NICK LEFT, he mulled everything over in his mind. Geraldine had been a penny-pincher. She'd been paying Maddie Cavanaugh only a couple dollars an hour to help her sort through her things.

So why had Maddie taken the job? Even babysitters made more than two dollars an hour. At least where he was from. Nick reminded himself to ask Maddie when he saw her again.

Arlene Evans seemed glad to see him. "I wanted to talk to you about Geraldine Shaw," Nick said as he sat down gingerly on the plastic-covered chair she offered him.

Arlene perched primly on the matching plastic-covered couch, her hands in her lap, a virtuous look on her face. He could hear the throb of the stereo coming from down the hall. At least one of her offspring apparently was home.

"Geraldine Shaw?" Arlene asked as if surprised he would ask about her.

"Did you know her long?"

"All my life."

"What was she like?"

Arlene took a deep breath and let it out slowly. "Cheap. The woman wouldn't spend a penny if she could get away with it."

"Maybe she didn't have it to spend," he said. "I heard her husband Ollie died last summer and didn't have any life insurance."

Arlene scoffed. "He left her well-off enough. Ollie was just like her, had the first dime he ever made. Tightfisted he was." She leaned toward him conspiratorially. "Geraldine came from old money back East. She and Ollie *had* money. Hoarders, that's what they were. Didn't trust banks either." She nodded knowingly.

"Are you saying they buried their money in the backyard?"

She smiled. "Maybe. Or hid it in that house. Never invited anyone over. Stayed to themselves. Who knows what's hidden over there?"

He could see Arlene going over there at night digging up the floorboards looking for the loot. Was there loot? Nick doubted it. Just a rumor that someone, probably Arlene, had started. And just such a rumor could have gotten Geraldine Shaw killed.

"I know for a fact that Mrs. Shaw died almost broke," Nick said.

Arlene smiled. "She just wanted everyone to think that was the case. Don't let anyone kid you, Geraldine Shaw didn't look all that bright, but she was a smart one."

"If she was so smart then how is it she managed to eat the only poisoned macaroon at the party?" It gave him an immense amount of pleasure to see Arlene Evans at a loss for words. Her mouth opened and closed like a guppy's, but nothing was coming out for a full thirty seconds.

"Poisoned?"

He nodded. "I was wondering if you had any idea who might have wanted her dead?"

"Who?" She sucked in a breath, then expelled it in a rush. "I'll tell you who." She glanced down the hallway toward what he assumed were her son's and daughters' rooms in the direction where the music boomed behind a closed door.

"Yes?" he asked.

Arlene looked a little guilty before she said, "Maddie Cavanaugh. I hate to say it about my son's fiancée, but I overheard Maddie and Geraldine arguing outside the community center right before the party."

"About what?"

"A missing diamond bracelet. Geraldine was convinced that Maddie had taken it. Maddie, of course, swore she hadn't." Arlene made a face. "I tried to get the truth out of her later."

When he'd caught the two of them behind the center.

"I told her I wouldn't have a thief in my family. I threatened to tell Bo."

"Did you?" he asked.

Arlene glanced back down the hall. "I couldn't keep something like that from him. He's my *son*. You probably heard they had a huge fight later. Bo hasn't said whether or not they'd broken up for good, but he's been in his room ever since except for meals."

"He doesn't have a job?"

She looked indignant. "He helps his father run this place when his father needs him."

Nick nodded. The kid seldom helped out. A mama's boy. "Can you tell me where you were when Geraldine collapsed?" Nick asked.

Arlene frowned. "I was outside with you."

"I believe you'd returned to the center. Someone saw you at the dessert table with your daughters."

"Then why did you ask me?" Arlene snapped. "I can't remember. It was all so traumatic. My son's engagement party of all places for her to die." She shook her head as though she couldn't believe Geraldine's gall.

"Do you have any idea what Geraldine might have eaten just before she collapsed?"

"How should I know what she ate?"

"Someone saw your daughters pass down the last macaroon possibly to you," he said.

"Me?" She shook her head.

"Don't you like macaroons?"

"I love them, but I was waiting for Laci to refill the plate. I didn't want that old stale one. I was glad when Geraldine took it." She sniffed as if there were a bad smell in the air. "Frankly, Laci has a lot to learn about baking. Macaroons should be moist, not wet, slightly rounded and never have almond flavoring in them."

"What makes you think the cookie had almond flavoring in it?"

She smiled pitying. "You're new here. You don't know that I am considered the best cook in the county." She motioned to a glassed-in cabinet that he hadn't noticed. It was full of blue ribbons.

"I *know* my cooking," she said with a nod. "Anyway, I smelled almond flavoring as Geraldine took it."

"Your daughter seemed to like the macaroons," he said.

"You're mistaken. Charlotte wouldn't touch a macaroon and Bo's allergic to coconut."

"Your other daughter. Violet."

"Oh, her." She did an eye roll. "Violet will eat anything. I've tried to teach her to cook…." She lifted a brow as if to say it was hopeless.

"You're also teaching your son's fiancée to cook, I understand. Maddie?"

Another eye roll. "Not everyone is capable of cooking. There is a talent to it."

"Your daughter Charlotte, is she a good cook?"

"Charlotte?" She let out a laugh. "She won't need to learn to cook. She'll do fine on her looks alone because she'll marry well."

Nick tried not to show his distaste for Arlene's theories.

"What are *you* looking for in a wife?" Arlene asked.

He chuckled uncomfortably. "I'm *not* looking."

"You're a handsome man. Too old for Charlotte, but there is always Violet or other single women in the area you might be interested in. I can sign you up for my Internet Meet-a-Mate business. It only takes a minute—"

"No thanks." He got to his feet, wanting to clear out as soon as possible. "What kind of poisons do you keep in the place?"

It was his lucky day. He'd caught Arlene Evans speechless twice in a row. Unfortunately nothing lasted long.

"How can you even ask something like that?" Arlene snapped. "Of course I don't have any poisons in this house, Deputy."

"Of course," he said as he moved to the door to leave.

"If you change your mind about the Meet-a-Mate," Arlene called from her porch, "you just let me know. First month free!"

He drove off as if heading for a fire and decided to run by Geraldine Shaw's house. The attorney had told him that the women from the community had been in the house earlier that day to take care of a few things.

There was safety in numbers so he didn't think he'd find the floorboards dug up where someone had been searching for hidden loot.

But he did worry about what he wouldn't find. A missing diamond bracelet. The attorney had gathered up the rest of Geraldine's jewelry. It was to be turned over to Maddie Cavanaugh once the estate was settled. There was no diamond bracelet.

What disturbed Nick was the fact that as far as he knew, the only person who'd spent much time in the house with Geraldine Shaw was Maddie Cavanaugh. So who else could have taken the bracelet? Unless it had just been misplaced.

He parked his pickup in the back and entered through the rear. He'd been dumbfounded to find out that no one in Whitehorse or most of rural Montana locked their doors.

The house had an old smell that went with the furnishings. It was cool and dark inside and resembled some museums he'd been in. He went from room to room trying to get a feel for Geraldine Shaw. The drapes were old but clean, the sheets on her bed threadbare, her clothing matronly and dated, the cupboard filled mostly with home-canned items from her garden.

Arlene had been right about one thing. Geraldine Shaw lived frugally. But because she had to? Or because she was a skinflint as Arlene and probably the rest of the town believed?

He heard the creak of a footfall on the front steps and slipped back into the shadows as the front door groaned open. He'd thought there might be visitors—but not until dark.

The door closed, then the sound of tentative footsteps grew closer. Nick would have expected Maddie to show up here. Or Arlene Evans.

So he was more than a little surprised when the intruder turned out to be the last person he'd expected.

He stepped out, startling Laney Cavanaugh. She slapped a hand over her heart, both surprised and guilty looking.

"Hello," he said, unable to hide his grin. Laney made the cutest criminal.

"What are you doing here?" she demanded.

"Funny, but that was what I was just about to ask you."

She reddened, glancing around as if there would be something in the room that could save her.

"You're not interfering in my investigation, are you, Miss Cavanaugh?"

She straightened to her full height, her expression resolute. "You are *investigating* people I care about."

He nodded. "Your cousin Maddie is hiding something." He could see she wanted to argue that, but didn't even try. "Why don't you tell me what you're doing here."

"I was by earlier with the rest of the community women to see what I could do to help," she said. "I left my sweater here."

She picked up a pale blue sweater from the arm of a rocker by the window.

Was it her sweater? Or was she just fast on her feet under pressure? He couldn't tell. She was that cool.

But given the way she'd entered the house, he'd say she was fast on her feet. Not that he didn't like that about her.

"That color goes well with your eyes," he said, smiling as he stepped closer and caught a whiff of perfume.

Laney, the times he'd been around her, smelled like fresh air and sunshine. The perfume, he realized, was coming from the blue sweater she had over her arm. How had Glen Whitaker described it? Old flowers.

"What is that scent?" he asked, thinking this wasn't the first time he'd smelled it. Arlene Evans's house had a faint hint of it. In fact, he would have sworn he'd seen Violet Evans a couple of days ago in a blue sweater just like this one.

Laney frowned. "What scent?"

"The perfume on your sweater."

Some of the cool left those emerald eyes of hers. She raised the sweater to her nose and sniffed. "Lavender."

Chapter Seven

Laney didn't like the look in Nick's eyes. It was as if he knew something she didn't. Worse, she was awful at this deceptive stuff. Or maybe she just didn't like withholding evidence. Especially from Nick.

"I have a confession," she blurted. "Geraldine Shaw stopped by the house right before the party. She'd misplaced a diamond bracelet. She thought Maddie had it and was upset."

He nodded. "So where is this bracelet?"

"That's just it. No one knows."

"You asked Maddie?"

She'd tried to get Maddie to open up to her after her interrogation in Nick's patrol car in front of the house. But Maddie, clearly upset, had said she needed to find Bo and had left in a rush.

"Maddie swears she left it in the jewelry box with the other items Geraldine had planned to sell and I believe her," Laney said with more force than she really felt. Something was going on with Maddie.

Laney had sensed it from the moment she'd seen her cousin. With each passing day, Laney was becoming more concerned that Maddie was in serious trouble.

"Can you describe this diamond bracelet?" Nick asked.

"I can do better than that." Laney handed him the snapshots Geraldine had had Maddie take and send copies to the antique jeweler.

"The rest of the jewelry is accounted for?"

She nodded.

He took the photo of the diamond bracelet and put it in his pocket. "Any more confessions?"

She met his dark eyes, tempted to confess that she'd wanted to kiss him from the moment she'd met him. "I think that about covers it. Except I was mistaken. This isn't my sweater." She hooked the blue sweater back over the arm of the rocker and turned to give him her best sheepish smile.

He seemed about to say something, then must have thought better of it. "No more investigating on your own, right?"

She didn't answer as she left. She didn't want to have to lie to him on top of everything else.

AFTER LANEY LEFT, NICK STOOD listening to her drive away. Clearly she hadn't come here for her sweater. But what? What would she have been looking for? The missing diamond bracelet? Or... He spied a drawer that was slightly cocked as if closed too quickly.

Stepping to it, he saw the dust was disturbed on

the cabinet as if someone had put a hand down on it. The handprint could have been Laney Cavanaugh's. It was that small, the fingers long and slim.

He pulled open the drawer, not surprised to find it contained Mrs. Shaw's personal financial records. Laney Cavanaugh was an accountant. He wondered what she might have found interesting in Geraldine's records.

As he started to leave, he had a thought. In the kitchen he found a clean trash bag under the sink. He put the sweater smelling of lavender in the bag and closed the top. If he was right, Glen Whitaker would recognize the scent.

He was anxious to get back to his office, to get the photo of the diamond bracelet on the wire. He was counting on whoever stole the bracelet to have pawned it as quickly as possible thinking that was safer than hanging on to it—especially after Geraldine Shaw dropped dead.

But as he drove by the community center, he noticed that the door was cracked open. Since he'd asked Titus to keep the place locked until the investigation was over, the door shouldn't have been open. There was no car parked out front, but he'd noticed a trail behind the center that led down to more parking at the bottom of the hill.

He slowed to a stop, parked at the edge of the road and walked back. As he neared, he heard a thud, as if someone had bumped against something inside the center. *Someone* was definitely in there.

He climbed the steps and eased the door open, peering into the dim cool darkness. From what he could see, everything was just as it had been the day of the murder sans the food.

He pushed the door open farther and stepped in.

Laney Cavanaugh stood at the end of the table where the desserts had been during the engagement party. She had her hands on her hips, her head tilted to one side. He could hear her muttering to herself.

He smiled, shaking his head. She hadn't exactly taken his warning about staying out of his investigation, now had she?

He thought about arresting her. He also thought about kissing her. The latter had the most appeal.

"And we meet again."

She jumped, spinning around, guilt written all over her face. "I was just—"

"Looking for your sweater? No, that's right, you found it at Geraldine Shaw's. But then it turned out not to be yours after all. I hope you at least found what you were looking for here. And please don't insult my intelligence with another story about a missing item of clothing."

She met his gaze. "Fine. I'm trying to find out who killed Geraldine Shaw so I can clear my sister."

He liked honesty. Hell, he liked this woman and found himself liking her more all the time. "I thought we'd already had this discussion. I'm the one who's going to find out who killed Geraldine Shaw. You were the one who was going to stay out of it. At least that's the way I remember it."

"I can't stay out of it. You don't know these people. I do. I know this town. I know its history."

He shook his head, afraid he knew what was coming.

"You need my help."

He smiled at that, tempting though it was. "I'm an officer of the law." He didn't add that he'd had more experience than he wanted to admit with murder. And an even closer brush with cyanide poisoning.

She said nothing, but still had that determined look in her eyes.

"You realize there's a law against impeding an investigation."

Determination brought her chin up. "You can arrest me if you don't like it."

What he liked was the idea of taking her back to town, but not to jail.

"I can help," she said, hesitated, then added, "I found Geraldine Shaw's financial records."

Yeah, so he'd discovered. He raised a brow though, curious what she'd made of what she'd found.

"She'd been withdrawing a thousand dollars a month in cash out of her savings account for the last year."

Which probably explained why Geraldine's savings account had less than a hundred dollars in it now.

"Blackmail?" he asked.

Laney shrugged then grinned. "You're the officer of the law here."

He shook his head at her, unable not to grin. "Arlene Evans thinks Geraldine hid thousands of dollars in her house."

"That's a rumor that's been going around for years." She shook her head. "They weren't poor, but they weren't rich either. Like most of the people who live in and around here, they lived off the land and made a living. No one around here gets rich. Or lives extravagantly."

"So what would anyone have to blackmail her about?" he asked.

"Your guess is as good as mine."

He took off his hat and scratched his head. "I'm sorry, where does your knowledge of these people and this community come in again?"

She glared at him. "I do have several theories about the murder if you're interested. It's one reason I stopped by here."

He put his hat back on, pushed back the brim and crossed his arms as he leaned against the wall. "I can't wait to hear them."

Laney ignored his sarcasm. She could put up with a lot to save her sister. And her cousin, because like him, she feared Maddie was somehow involved in all this.

But putting up with Nick Rogers also meant ignoring the way her heart took off at a gallop when he was around. He seemed to fill any space he was in, changed the air pressure and the temperature. Made her body feel hypersensitive as if just his nearness was a caress across her bare skin.

What Nick Rogers did was remind her that she was a woman and it had been a long while since any man had done that.

"If the poison wasn't in the macaroons—which it wasn't since Laci baked them—then it had to have been added between the time she baked them and they ended up on this table," she said, corralling her thoughts.

He nodded. "Who took them from the house to the center?"

"Aunt Sarah, Maddie's mom, brought some of the baked goods, Laci and I brought the rest." Before he could ask, she added, "I personally loaded the macaroons." She met his gaze. "In case you're wondering, I didn't poison them."

"So you carried the macaroons in and left them on the back counter behind the tables. Laci put them on the table and Laci was the only one who had access to the rest, right?"

She hated to admit it. "Yes."

"So if Laci didn't put the poison in the cookie, then it had to be administered while the macaroons were on the table, right?" His dark eyes reminded her of this part of Montana, vast.

She shook her head. "Too sloppy. The killer couldn't chance being seen adding the poison to the cookie. So if you were the killer, what would you do?"

He shrugged. "Enlighten me."

"Bring your own macaroon with the poison already in it."

"Your sister's right about you. She said you had a very analytical mind."

She heard his words, not just the ones he spoke, but the ones he didn't as his gaze washed over her. She felt heat flush her skin as she turned her back on him to study the counter behind the table. She hated that her behavior probably only made her look guilty.

Better him think that, she reasoned, than what she really had on her mind.

NICK STUDIED HER BACKSIDE, liking the set of her shoulders, the determined tilt of her head, the way her jeans fit her. The fact that she was hiding something from him only intrigued him as much as the woman herself. Since lunch she had changed to jeans and a sleeveless blouse, both dark blue. He suspected this was her investigating outfit.

"Nice theory," he said as he debated what to do about Laney Cavanaugh. She was definitely too smart for her own good. The killer was bound to find out that she was doing some investigating on her own. From what she'd said, she wasn't going to give up until she found out the truth.

And that was the problem. This was way too dangerous for her to be nosing around in. Worse, she could go too far—and find not only the killer—but also uncover things about Nick Rogers and what he was really doing here.

The problem was that warning her to stay out of his investigation was a waste of breath. She was right. She knew the locals, she knew the area and maybe even harder to accept, he needed her.

He also needed to keep an eye on her. For his own protection if not hers. Mostly, keeping an eye on Laney Cavanaugh was exactly what he wanted to do.

"So the killer baked one macaroon with almond extract and poison in it?" he asked, having a few theories of his own, but curious to see what she'd come up with.

She turned around to look at him. Her eyes were that clear cool-water mix of greens. "Almond extract?"

He nodded. "Arlene Evans said she smelled it in the cookie."

"Laci would never have changed the recipe that way. She's a purest about old family recipes. Our macaroons don't have almond extract in them."

He loved the way she not only defended her sister, but also the family recipe. "How did the killer know Laci was making macaroons?"

"Someone told her they were Bo's favorite," she said.

"But I talked to Arlene. Bo is allergic to coconut."

"The intended victim would have had to have liked macaroons."

He smiled and nodded. "Apparently Geraldine liked macaroons. And Arlene—although she says she prefers her own recipe. And Violet apparently was a big fan of the cookies."

"The macaroon would have to be identical to the others," she said more to herself than to him.

"Where did she get what your sister said was an old family recipe, then?"

"The Whitehorse Sewing Circle's cookbook. My grandmother donated the recipe to raise money for the center."

He nodded. Of course she had. "You're right. You know these people, this place. I'm out of my league."

She smiled. "I really doubt that."

He saw Laney consider him, the steel of her gaze and spine not quite as severe. "You don't think Laci poisoned Geraldine."

He shook his head.

She seemed to relax a little more, softening as she did. He felt a pull stronger than gravity toward her and fought it as a drowning man fought water.

"Have dinner with me." The words were out before he could call them back.

"Thanks but I don't think that would be a good idea."

"Why not?"

She studied him openly. "Wouldn't it look bad if you were fraternizing with a suspect? I am a suspect, right?"

"I can't see you poisoning anyone."

"Really? Didn't I hear somewhere that poison is a woman's weapon?"

She was definitely a woman.

"If you were the killer, you wouldn't leave anything to chance," he said.

"True," she agreed.

"This killer couldn't be sure her intended victim got the cookie," he pointed out.

"Unless she gave the victim the cookie and Geraldine was the intended victim."

"Good point. Except neither of us believes Geraldine was the intended victim."

She smiled again. "How do you know that?"

"Because the only person who benefited from Geraldine Shaw's death was Maddie."

"And the Whitehorse Sewing Circle."

"I got the impression from talking to the lawyer that the women of the sewing circle had no idea Geraldine was leaving them anything," he said.

She nodded. "I was there. Everyone was shocked."

"So that leaves Maddie," he said quietly. "It would appear she killed Geraldine to cover up the thief of the diamond bracelet."

Laney shook her head. "The bracelet went missing the day of the party. Maddie didn't have time to bake a poison macaroon."

"Unless she'd been planning to rip off Geraldine all along," he pointed out. "Maddie was the only one who knew about the jewelry, knew Geraldine would be sending it to Billings to that antique dealer soon, so she had to act fast. Her party was the perfect place."

"Why not just conk Geraldine on the head and take the jewelry then? Wouldn't that be much easier? She could say the woman fell. And no one knew about the jewelry except Geraldine and Maddie. No one would know what was missing."

He smiled at Laney. He liked her mind. "Good points. Also, Arlene says Maddie can't cook. Plus Maddie was outside with me. Bo came and got her. She didn't have time to slip Geraldine a cookie."

"So you were just playing devil's advocate?" Laney demanded. Anger flashed in all that emerald-green.

"Just seeing if there were any holes in my logic."

She glared at him. "You could have told me up front that you didn't believe Laci *or* Maddie were guilty."

"I didn't say Maddie wasn't guilty. I just don't think she killed Geraldine Shaw."

"You think she took that diamond bracelet?"

"Maybe. If not, she knows who did," he said. "As for the murder, I think the killer decided to take advantage of the party." And if that made Laci Cavanaugh look guilty in the process, so much the better.

"Any ideas who could have baked the counterfeit cookie?" he asked.

"Anyone who might have a Whitehorse Sewing Circle cookbook."

"Do you recall how many copies were printed?"

"Two hundred."

"That leaves it wide open." He let out a low whistle. "Remind me to get one before I leave."

"Are you planning to leave?" she asked, her gaze intent on him suddenly.

"Before I leave Old Town today," he said, catching himself. "They are still for sale, aren't they?"

She shook her head. "But I could probably get you a copy sometime."

Was it just his imagination that she seemed to be eyeing him with suspicion? Probably.

But then again, the woman was sharp. He'd have to watch himself around her.

"So what now?" she asked.

He glanced at his watch. "Better decide where to go for dinner. Since you know the area…"

She shook her head, but she was smiling. "Have you been to the Tin Cup?"

AFTER NICK MADE LANEY PROMISE she wouldn't do any more snooping around in the case without him, he watched her drive off in the direction of home before he returned to Whitehorse. His first stop was his office to fax the photograph of the missing diamond bracelet to pawn shops and cop departments in a two-hundred-mile area.

Next he dropped by the *Milk River Examiner* office.

Glen Whitaker looked up from his desk as Nick came in carrying the trash bag with the sweater inside.

"I have something I was hoping you might be able to help me with," Nick said. "There's a scent on this sweater and I wondered…" He opened the bag and held it for the reporter to take a whiff.

"That's it!" Glen cried, then lowered his voice. There was no one else in the office, but Glen must have known from experience that walls sometimes had big ears. "That's the smell that was on my clothing after I was attacked. What is it?"

"Lavender."

Glen wrinkled his nose. "That smell makes me a little sick."

Nick wondered just what had happened to Glen before he'd regained consciousness beside that road.

"Why would I smell lavender after my attack?" Glen asked.

"I'm working on that," Nick said and, closing the bag with the sweater, headed for the sheriff's department.

Harvey T. Brown had filed an assault report. The deputy who'd handled the complaint had written down that Brown remembered smelling something sweet, like maybe flowers or perfume, or "those things people put in their cars to cover up odors." He'd also glimpsed a baseball bat just before he'd been hit.

Nick drove the bagged sweater out to Brown's place north of town. Harvey T. Brown was a large man with a beer belly and a bald spot.

"That could be the smell," Brown said from his

recliner. He recoiled at the scent much as Glen Whitaker had, lying back in his chair. "Was there some of that kind of flower that smelled like that growing outside the bar?"

Nick had to shake his head. "I think there's a good possibility the person wielding the baseball bat was a woman."

"No way," Brown said shooting to his feet. He marched into the kitchen, opened the fridge and took out a can of beer. "You tell anyone in this town that I was beat up by a woman and so help me I will—"

"Take it easy," Nick told him. "It's just a theory."

"It better not be one I ever hear again," Brown said, sitting back down in his recliner and popping the top on his beer. He chugged most of the can, belched and glared at Nick. "I was beat up by some big burly guy. I didn't smell nothing. Got it?"

"Got it."

"I LIKE THIS PLACE," NICK SAID later when he and Laney were sitting in the dining room at the country club overlooking the golf course. Mostly he liked the company he was with.

"Surprised Whitehorse has a golf course?" she asked smiling across the table at him. "There's two in the area. Another one out at Sleeping Buffalo." She was wearing a pale green dress that brought out the tropical-green of her eyes. The dress seemed to float over her curves as gently as a caress. She smelled good, too. Something fruity that went with the summer evening.

Nick knew he would never forget that scent. Or this night. No matter what happened in the future.

During dinner they talked about their childhoods, Laney's growing up in Old Town Whitehorse, Nick's edited story of growing up in a large Italian family. They had the place pretty much to themselves since it was a weekday.

The food was wonderful, the view breathtaking as the sun set in a glow of colors and night shadows drifted over the place like a warm breeze.

"I'm serious about you being careful," he said as the evening drew to an end. She'd insisted on driving in from Old Town, saying she had to visit her grandmother in the hospital anyway and it would save him the trip out and back.

As the restaurant emptied out completely, he reached across the table and put his hand over hers, something he'd wanted to do all evening.

"I'm always careful." Her gaze met his. "Well, almost always." She was flirting with him, he was pretty sure of it.

He was treading on thin ice. But what worried him was that she didn't seem in the least bit afraid. Not of flirting with him. Or looking for a killer. Both were much more dangerous than she imagined.

He drew his hand back. "There's a killer out there and until we find out why Geraldine is dead—"

She shook her head. "Don't you think what we

have to find out is who the killer really wanted dead since neither of us believes the intended victim was Geraldine Shaw?"

He smiled. "But neither of us has any evidence to substantiate that."

"I was there, remember? I didn't see her take a bite of the macaroon or collapse, but when I got through the crowd to her, I remember hearing someone crying, 'no, oh no.'"

He could argue that "no, oh no" wasn't conclusive evidence of anything but shock or surprise when Geraldine had collapsed.

"The other odd thing was that I couldn't see one of Geraldine's arms with everyone crowded around her," Laney said. "But I could see that she was struggling as if someone had hold of her wrist. When you moved everyone back, I saw that her fingers holding the cookie were white they were gripped so tightly and there were several red marks on her palm where it appeared someone had tried to pry her fingers open."

"The killer was probably trying to get the evidence to destroy it," he said.

"Maybe," she agreed. "Or maybe the killer was upset and trying to get the cookie back because she'd just killed the wrong person."

"She?"

Laney nodded. "The voice I heard was definitely a woman's. And wouldn't a man have been able to pry Geraldine's fingers open?"

He chuckled and took a sip of his drink. Brains and beauty, a deadly combination. He hoped the fact that the killer had used cyanide was just a terrible coincidence, because otherwise this Nancy Drew sitting across the table from him might just stumble on the truth not only about the killer, but him as well. That should have frightened him more than it did. Hell, the truth was, he wanted to tell her everything. He hated lying to her.

He took a sip of his drink, dropping his gaze, as he tried to talk some sense into himself. Telling anyone was like signing his own death warrant. What the hell was he thinking?

"You like women to think you're shy, don't you?" she said studying him.

He looked up at her, meeting her gaze, and grinned. "Oh, that's real. At least with you."

She cocked a brow at him.

"You're a scary woman."

"You do look frightened."

He laughed. She didn't know how close to the truth she'd come.

Chapter Eight

Nick couldn't help thinking about Laney. For a lot of reasons. Her grandfather Titus dropped off a copy of the Whitehorse Sewing Circle cookbook first thing the next morning.

Nick found her grandmother's recipe and read through it, then called Laney. "Would you have to be a pretty good cook to make your grandmother's macaroons?" he asked. "They don't look that easy."

"They aren't."

"Then our killer is a better than average cook, whose victim likes coconut, right?" He heard her smile even over the phone. "Any suggestions who to talk to?"

"Pretty near every woman in Old Town Whitehorse," she said with a laugh. "Haven't you heard? They're the best cooks in the county. At least according to Arlene Evans and she has the blue ribbons to prove it."

"Yes, she mentioned that. And she was closest to

the poisoned macaroon when Geraldine ate it." He
fiddled for a moment with a pen on his desk. "I had
a good time last night at dinner."

"Me, too." Her voice was soft and low. He imagined her still in her pj's. Silk, the color of her eyes. The
image of emerald-green silk draped over that body—

"Would you mind telling me what you're wearing
right now?"

"What?" She laughed. "You aren't serious."

He needed a good dose of reality. "Yes, I am."

Silence, then a small embarrassed laugh. "Well,
I have on a pair of old jeans and one of my grandfather's flannel shirts and a ratty pair of tennis shoes
I found at the back of the closet. All of the above are
covered in paint."

"What color paint?"

She laughed again. "White. I'm painting the
picket fence out front." She lowered her voice. "So
what does my attire do for you?"

He sat up, tossing down the pen. "It makes me
realize that I have to see you again."

Another smile in her voice as she said, "Good."

"Great. Oh, and, no investigating without me,
right?"

"Right. Just painting."

"Good girl." He hung up still smiling. He caught
his reflection in the window. "Wipe that stupid smile
off your face," he told himself. "You look like a fool.
Worse, you're acting like one."

He forced himself to turn his thoughts to the

murder of Geraldine Shaw. The plan had been ama-teurish at best. A plan born of passion—not preci-sion. Passion meant anger and anger was a detriment to the killer—and an advantage for the lawman. So who was angry with Geraldine Shaw?

Apparently no one.

What did that leave him? An angry killer who had failed at poisoning his intended victim? *Her* in-tended victim, he corrected, remembering what Laney had said. Going with Laney's theory, the killer would also need at least a passing knowledge of poison—and cooking. And a motive.

The call came as he was leaving his office.

"Deputy Rogers? This is Clyde Banner. I own the Pawn and Go in Great Falls. I think I have the diamond bracelet you're looking for. I just took a digital photo of it and e-mailed it to your office."

Nick sat down and called up the Internet. There was an e-mail from Pawn and Go. He clicked on it. A photo came up. Geraldine Shaw's bracelet.

"That's it," he told Clyde. "Can you tell me who pawned it?"

"Well, that's what's kind of curious about the pawn slip. The guy who came in said his name was Nick Rogers."

Cute. Someone playing games with him.

"You weren't suspicious?" Nick asked.

"I'm always suspicious, but unless it comes up on a hot sheet…"

"What did this Nick Rogers look like?" he asked.

"Young. Nineteen, twenty. Brown hair, brown eyes. Good-looking kid. Clean cut. He looked legit enough. Hell, he was driving a nice car."

"How nice?" Nick asked and listened as Clyde Banner described Bo Evans's car to a T. "I might need you to ID the kid."

"No problem. I'll put the bracelet in the safe. I assume you'll have someone pick it up?"

"Thanks." Nick hung up and sat for a moment before he dialed Laney's number. "I need to talk to your cousin. Want to ride along?"

"I'll be ready when you get here," she said, obviously hearing something in his voice that warned her it wasn't good news.

Maddie was surprised to see them. Her car was in the yard. Her mother's was gone. From the look on her face, she wished she hadn't answered the door. She stood in the doorway, looking from one to the other, looking scared.

"Mind if we come in?" Nick asked.

"I was just going to town to—"

"This won't take long," he said.

Maddie looked to her cousin. Laney nodded and they stepped into the cool clean house.

The place smelled of lemon cleaner. There was no dust on the end table next to the couch, no magazines or newspapers cluttering up the coffee table. Nick was surprised there wasn't any plastic on the furniture.

He took a seat on the couch. Laney hugged her cousin and sat on one of the chairs. Maddie stood as if lost. She ran her hands along the sides of her jeans, clearly nervous.

"Can I get you something to drink?" she asked, flashing them a nervous smile. "You both look so serious."

"Sit down, Maddie," Nick said.

She dropped into a chair, her blue eyes wide with fear. "Has something happened?"

"The photographs you took of Geraldine Shaw's jewelry? Who did you show them to?" Nick asked.

Maddie swallowed, her eyes swimming in tears. "Nobody."

"You didn't show them to your fiancé?"

One tear broke loose and cascaded down her freckled cheek. "I…"

"Maddie, I found Geraldine's diamond bracelet. It was pawned at a shop in Great Falls. The clerk described Bo Evans as the person who pawned it."

She began to cry, shaking her head from side to side.

"Did you give him the bracelet?"

Her eyes widened in alarm. "No," she cried. "I swear. I told him about the bracelet, but I never dreamed he'd…" Her words were lost in tears.

Laney handed her cousin a tissue.

"You and Bo had a fight after his mother told him that Geraldine Shaw thought you'd taken the diamond bracelet," Nick said.

Maddie looked up at him, tears cascading down her face, but no sound coming out of her now.

"Didn't he mention then that he'd taken the bracelet?" Nick asked. "Surely, he wouldn't let his mother think you were a thief and not defend you."

Maddie began to sob openly in answer. Just as Nick had suspected, Bo hadn't cleared things up for his mother or his fiancée.

"Bo's going to be arrested," Nick told her. "You might want to rethink your engagement to him."

"No, you can't arrest him," Maddie cried through her tears. "Can't you just give him a warning? Arlene will blame me."

"Arlene? Why would she blame you?" Laney demanded.

"She just will."

Nick studied the young woman. "Arlene's the one who put those bruises on your arms, isn't she?"

Maddie looked down, plucking at her sleeves to hide them. "I'm just a klutz."

"Maddie, stop covering for that family," Laney said, going to her cousin and kneeling down in front of her.

"She's right," Nick said. "If this is the way they treat you now, trust me, it will only get worse once you're married to Bo."

"But I love Bo," Maddie wailed. "I can't live without him. No one will love me like Bo does."

Laney handed her cousin more tissues and put her arm around her. "Come stay with me and Laci. We won't let anyone hurt you anymore."

Maddie sounded like a wounded animal, her cries heartbreaking, as Nick left Laney to take care of her cousin.

AT THE EVANS HOUSE, Nick could hear music blaring as he knocked on the screen door. Arlene's truck was gone, but Bo's souped-up ride was sitting out front.

Nick banged on the door frame. "Bo," he called loudly. No response. He banged again.

Violet appeared from the semidarkness inside, giving him a start. She must have been sitting in the darkened living room, the drapes drawn. He hadn't heard the creak of plastic as she'd gotten up. Nor had she made a sound as she'd approached.

"Mother's not here," she said meekly. Her face was paler than he remembered and there were dark circles under her eyes. "She's at the doctor's."

"She's not feeling well?"

She shook her head.

"Your brother around?"

Violet seemed to hesitate as if tempted to lie. It surprised him she might lie for her brother. Nick had gotten the impression she wasn't close to her siblings.

"Could you tell him I'm here?" Nick said, opening the screen door and stepping in.

"I'm not sure he's home." Violet was forced to take a step back.

"Why don't I try his room," Nick said. He moved past her across the living room and down the hall, following the sound of a heavy-metal band with no talent for songwriting. The monotonous beat made his teeth ache.

He pounded on Bo's bedroom door.

"Go away!"

Nick opened the door. Bo looked up from where he was sprawled on his rumpled bed. Apparently Arlene hadn't felt well enough to make her son's bed this morning.

"What do you want?" he yelled over the racket coming from the stereo.

Nick stepped over to the stereo and shut if off.

"What do you think you're doing?" Bo demanded.

"Reading you your rights."

"What?" He sat up.

The room had a funky smell. The kid was a slob and it took all Nick's control not to tell him so.

"You have the right to remain—"

"Whoa. Don't you have to tell me why you're arresting me first?" Bo demanded, only the slight squeak in his voice giving away his concern.

"Guess," Nick said as he pulled out his cuffs.

"I don't know anything about that bracelet."

"Did I say anything about a bracelet, Bo?"

"Maddie. She gave it to me. She's the one who made me do it."

"Your mother might believe that story, but it isn't going to fly with me," Nick said. "And if it were true, wouldn't a fiancé try to cover for the woman he loved? You're despicable. Now get on your feet."

He saw Bo look toward the door as if gauging his chances of escaping.

"*Please,* try to resist arrest," Nick said. "There is nothing I would like better than to kick your ass."

Bo Evans scowled as he stood and held out his hands. "You're going to regret this. My mother will have your job," he said, but his voice broke.

Nick shoved Bo toward the door. Violet watched as Nick took her brother away, her gaze unreadable.

As he shoved Bo into the back of the patrol car, Charlotte Evans drove up. She glanced at her brother in cuffs in the backseat, then at Nick. With apparent disinterest, she got out and started toward the house.

"Charlotte, do you know where I can find your mother?" Nick asked her.

"At the hospital," she said, sounding surprised. "Didn't Bo tell you? Mother took a nasty spill down the basement stairs last night. She broke her arm and has a concussion."

IT RAINED THAT SATURDAY, the day of Geraldine Shaw's funeral. Laney stood on the hillside overlooking Old Town. Only a few black umbrellas huddled around the grave site as Titus stood with Bible in hand and said a few kind words over Geraldine's grave.

The low turnout could have been because of the gray rainy day. But Laney knew it had more to do with the fact that most everyone didn't know Geraldine well.

"Dust to dust…" Laney's grandfather's words were lost to her as she noticed Deputy Nick Rogers standing back in the darkness of the trees some distance away. He seemed to be watching the people around the grave.

All of the women of the Whitehorse Sewing Circle were there either out of respect or because Geraldine had left them her house and property. It wouldn't amount to a lot of money in this part of Montana, but the sentiment was definitely there.

Even Arlene Evans had shown up wearing a cast on her broken arm like a badge of honor. Her bruised face had healed to purple and yellow. She'd told everyone in the county how the top step on the basement stairs had been loose and with Bo in jail for a crime he didn't commit and her husband too busy with farming to fix it, she'd fallen.

Most everyone knew Arlene had fallen before Bo had been arrested. But Arlene had ridden the story like a dying horse.

Flanking her on each side were her two daughters. Violet in a black cape reminiscent of Dracula. Charlotte in a little black dress and heels with a knitted shawl draped around her as if on a fashion runway. Arlene wore a hat with a short black veil that hid most of the damage to her face. She sniffed loudly every few minutes. Laney suspected the sniffing had more to do with her son's arrest than Geraldine Shaw's funeral service.

Laney noticed that Arlene had made a point of not

standing anywhere near Maddie. Instead Maddie stood at the edge of the grave next to her cousins. She cried softly, her head down, her reddish-blond hair wet from the rain. Laney had tried to get her to stay under the large umbrella she'd brought, but Maddie wouldn't hear of it.

She stood in the rain as if it would wash away her pain.

"I can't live without Bo," she'd cried whenever Laci or Laney had tried to talk to her about his arrest and the engagement. "You don't understand. I'll never find anyone who loves me as much as Bo."

Laney had argued that if Bo loved her, he wouldn't have taken Geraldine Shaw's diamond bracelet and pawned it, letting Maddie take the rap.

"He wanted the money for our wedding," Maddie had cried.

"If he needed money, he should have gotten a job," Laney had said.

Maddie had burst into tears and run from the room.

"You could have been a little more diplomatic," Laci had said to her and gone to Maddie.

Laney wanted to shake some sense into her cousin, but she feared that love was truly blind, deaf and painfully stupid.

The thought sent her gaze in the direction of Deputy Sheriff Nick Rogers. She hadn't seen him in days. Maybe more troubling was the fact that he hadn't even tried to kiss her the night they'd gone to dinner.

He'd walked her out to her car and they'd stood under a canopy of stars, a breeze stirring the leaves on a nearby tree, the summer evening rich with warmth.

She'd given him every opportunity and yet he'd hung back as if, as he'd said, he was afraid. Afraid of what? she wondered as she studied him. He didn't seem like a man who scared easily.

Her grandfather closed his Bible, his words dying off.

"If anyone would like to say a few words…" Titus looked around the small group. "Then—"

"I want to say something," Maddie blurted out. She swallowed, her eyes wet from the rain and tears, her face red and swollen from all the crying she'd been doing. "I didn't know Geraldine, not hardly at all. But she was nice to me. I'm sorry she's dead." With that she began to cry harder.

Titus signaled that the funeral service was over and everyone dispersed like dark seeds blown to the wind.

Laney watched them go. All except Nick. He seemed to be waiting for her. She walked to where he stood, his western hat catching most of the rain, that and the heavy boughs of the ponderosa pine he stood under.

"Hello," she said feeling strangely shy.

"Hello." He smiled at her. "I thought I should warn you, I think Arlene is going to get Bo sprung from jail."

Laney groaned.

"Maddie still determined to marry him?"

She nodded. "How can she not see what kind of man he is?"

Nick shook his head. "People see what they want." His dark eyes were intent on her. "I've missed you." The admission seemed to come hard for him. "Any chance I could take you to town for an early dinner and a show?"

"What's playing?" she asked.

"Whatever the Villa is showing this week. Does it matter?"

It didn't.

NICK HAD NEVER LIVED IN A TOWN that had only one theater. Not only that, the old-time theater screened only one show, and even that for only a few nights a week. But he loved the Villa. It was big and classic and reminded him of when he was a kid and his uncle Cosmos used to take him to matinees in a huge neighborhood theater with a balcony.

Those kinds of theaters were gone. Whitehorse's was one of the few left in Montana.

"It would be like a real date. I'd pick you up and take you home. I'd even buy you popcorn," he said, warming to the idea, hoping she would say yes.

"Buttered popcorn?" she asked.

He grinned. "You are a woman after my own heart."

"I guess it's a date then."

He felt as if the sun had come out as he walked

through the rain with her to her car. They agreed on a time and he stood in the downpour and watched her drive away, wishing things were different.

But the truth was he could be leaving any day.

Not to mention the fact that he was lying about who he was, where he was from, what he was doing here. Guilt pricked at his conscience. With each passing day, he hated that he was living a lie. It was why he'd made a point of avoiding Laney.

He didn't want to lie to her anymore.

But he also couldn't tell her the truth.

Just the thought turned the day gray and rainy again as he walked to his patrol car. He couldn't tell her. He couldn't tell anyone. He was on borrowed time. Any day he could get the call. Any day might be the last he ever saw Laney Cavanaugh. Or the day he came face-to-face again with Keller—and a bullet.

Chapter Nine

The rain had stopped as he'd started out of town. Nick couldn't believe how many accidents there'd been in the last few weeks in Old Town Whitehorse.

Arlene Evans had fallen down her stairs. Alice Miller had wrecked her car on the way out of town. Muriel Brown's house had caught fire. If her dog hadn't started barking, she might have died in her sleep. Fortunately, the fire had started in a trash can on her back porch and she'd been able to put it out before it had done any real damage.

There'd been too many near accidents for the size of the near ghost town. If he and Laney were right about Geraldine Shaw not being the intended victim, then maybe the killer was playing havoc with the town. Nick had the bad feeling it wasn't over. That the killer wouldn't be done until Old Town Whitehorse had another dead body on its hands.

He spotted Chaz and his dog Prince walking up the road near the Evans place. He drove down, turning around in the Evans yard, and rolled down his window as Prince came bounding over. The dog licked his hand, tongue lolling.

"Stolen any chickens lately?" Nick asked Prince.

"No, sir," Chaz answered for the dog. "I've been keeping a close eye on him. Just like you said."

Nick had seen the boy walking the dog most every day he'd been down here. New to the area, Chaz probably didn't have many friends. For one thing, there weren't a lot of kids his age around. The residents were older; the next generation had left. The few who had come back here were young, their children still in diapers.

Chaz put a protective hand on his dog's head as Charlotte Evans came roaring down the road to swing into her yard. She got out of her car, spotted Chaz and Prince and made a beeline for the dog. She was still dressed in her funeral outfit, black high heels and a skinny little black dress, but she'd ditched the shawl.

"What's your dog's name?" she asked with more enthusiasm than Nick had ever seen in her.

"Prince," Chaz said shyly.

"Prince," Charlotte repeated and smiled. "I like that. Can I pet him?"

Chaz nodded. Nick saw that the boy was taken with Charlotte. Not that he could blame him. A boy his age would see Charlotte as an attractive older woman.

"How's your mother doing?" Nick asked Charlotte.

"Fine. Violet had to take her back to the hospital. She has some kind of infection." She dismissed her mother and turned her attention to the dog. "Prince seems real nice," she said as the dog licked her hand and leaned against her leg. "We can't have a dog. Bo is allergic. He's allergic to *everything*."

Especially work, Nick thought.

"Would you like a glass of iced tea?" Charlotte asked Chaz. "Prince can have some water on the porch."

"Sure," Chaz said as he and Prince left Nick without a backward glance. As Nick pulled away, he saw both Chaz and Prince go into the house. So much for Bo's allergies.

Nick wasn't surprised when he returned to his office to find a call from the town judge.

"Arlene makes a good argument," the judge said when Nick returned his call. "She needs her boy at home right now. She can't drive and her husband is busy in the fields."

Nick realized he'd never seen her husband. He was beginning to wonder if Floyd Evans even existed.

"What I'm getting at," the judge continued, "is that this is Bo's first offense. I'm inclined to let him go home. He's promised to make restitution."

"You realize that the woman he stole the diamond bracelet from is dead and that Bo's fiancée inherited the bracelet," Nick pointed out. "I really doubt he'll make restitution to his fiancée."

"That's neither here nor there. I think the boy has learned his lesson," the judge said. "I've known Floyd and Arlene Evans all my life. Arlene's pretty much had to raise those kids by herself. You probably don't know it, but Bo used to be quite the athlete. He took the school to state both his junior and senior years."

Nick started to argue that the judge wouldn't be doing that family any favors releasing Bo.

"Arlene needs her son at home to help her," the judge said cutting him off. "Since this is Bo's first offense, I'm going to give him fifty hours of community service."

Nick heard in the judge's voice that it wouldn't do any good to argue further. Bo was a local boy. Nick wasn't. Bo was a good-looking kid who'd ride those two years of fame in high school as long as he could.

"I'll see that he gets home," Nick said.

"No need. His fiancée is here to pick him up," the judge said.

Maddie. Apparently Laney hadn't had any more luck convincing her that Bo wasn't the love of her life than Nick had.

"How is the investigation going?" Laney asked as she dredged a French fry through a lake of ketchup.

Nick looked up from his bacon cheeseburger. "Slow."

They'd picked up burgers, fries and shakes at the

Dairy Queen and taken them to a picnic table in Trafton Park near the Milk River. The leaves of the huge cottonwoods rustled overhead.

"I did some asking around about cyanide," she said between bites. "I guess they use it in mining."

"One use," he agreed. "Unfortunately, cyanide is used in everything from photography to metal cleaning. If you grind up enough chokecherry seeds, the cyanide in them will probably kill you. Cyanide is too common to probably ever track down the source."

Lancy couldn't help but be disappointed. She didn't want this hanging over her sister's head. Or her cousin's. They had to find out who had killed Geraldine Shaw and why.

"Don't worry, I'm not going to quit looking for the killer," he said as if reading her expression.

She smiled at him, wanting to reach across the table and cup his strong jaw. She knew the skin would feel warm and dry, a little rough with just the hint of his beard. She shivered.

"If you're cold we could—"

"No, I'm fine." She concentrated on her burger for a few moments. "You must find Montana very different from Texas, especially our area of the state."

He smiled as he met her gaze. He had the darkest eyes. "I like it here. I like the open country and the people. Everyone is so friendly."

She eyed him suspiciously. "You don't think we're all backwoodsy local yokels?"

He laughed and shook his head. "I find you all

charming and unique. Especially you." He grinned at her. "I like that it feels as if nothing has changed around here in the last hundred years."

She laughed. "It hasn't. And you're saying that's a good thing?"

"Yeah. It is. There's history here that you can feel. You know what I mean?"

She did. It was one reason she loved coming here every summer. Everyone knew everyone else and their families. Generation after generation had stayed to work the land; they'd planted deep roots; they had shared memories. She loved that feeling of belonging.

"Can I ask about your mother and father?"

She met his gaze. "There isn't much to tell. They fell in love in high school, got married young. My father was Russ Cherry. You know that big old empty house in Whitehorse?"

"The one that looks haunted?"

She winced. "I wouldn't be surprised if it was haunted. That house saw a lot of tragedy. My grandfather Cherry killed himself and my grandmother Cherry in that house. The place has been empty ever since."

"I'm so sorry," Nick said. "Your father…?"

"He and my mother had been childhood sweethearts. They married young and moved into the house Laci and I stay in every summer. My grandfather Titus built it for them out on the ranch as a wedding present. They hadn't been married long when they had me, then Laci, right after that."

"I'm sorry, if this is too painful—"

"No, it's like someone else's story since Laci and I were so young when it all happened. My father had gone into town a few weeks after the funeral. He was coming home. They said he'd been drinking. He rolled his pickup and was killed. My mother never got over his death, I guess. One day she just disappeared and was never seen again."

Nick reached across the table and took her hand. "You lost so many people in such a short time."

"Laci and I had Gramps and Gramma. They raised us. We were lucky really because we couldn't have asked for a more idyllic childhood. I wish you could have met my grandmother before her stroke. She was the most vibrant woman. Strong, determined homestead woman."

"Like her granddaughter."

She smiled at that. "I hope to be like my grandmother someday. But those will be huge shoes to fill."

"I have no doubt you'll make her proud."

She could hear the rustle of trees, smell fresh-cut grass and feel the slow, reassuring warmth of Nick's hand.

Then he drew back as he always did. "How is your cousin?" he asked, changing the subject.

"I haven't been able to talk to her." Laney hated to admit it. "When I call, I'm told she's out."

"You don't believe it?"

She shook her head. "Maddie's upset with me and Laci because we tried to talk her into breaking her engagement. I wasn't very diplomatic, I'm afraid."

He smiled knowingly. "I probably didn't use the best tack either. She's nineteen. Legally she can marry anyone she wants."

Laney let out a sigh. "I think she's just afraid that she will never love anyone the way she does Bo. I can understand that."

"Who was he?" Nick asked.

She blinked in surprise. "I...I..." She looked away. "A boy I met my first year at college. I thought he hung the moon."

"What happened?"

"Life," she said with a rueful laugh. "We were too young to make a lifetime commitment. We both went our separate ways. I heard he got a job in a large corporation back East and married the boss's daughter. It would never have worked for the two of us. That wasn't the life I wanted, and this," she said with the wave of her hand, "wasn't even close to what he wanted." She met Nick's nearly black gaze. "What about you?"

"My heart's been broken so many times I've lost count," he said.

"I seriously doubt that."

"It's true. Women always think they want the strong silent type until they realize that we're just dull."

She laughed, studying him as they finished eating in a companionable silence. Funny, but she was beginning to notice that he often didn't give her a straight answer. Almost as if he was afraid she'd get too close to the truth.

"We'd better get to the Villa," he said as he rose from the table. "I hope you left room for buttered popcorn." He collected the wrappers from their picnic and took them over to the large trash can.

Laney watched him go, thinking he was the sexiest man she'd ever met. And the most intriguing. But she couldn't ignore that underlying feeling that she would be smart not to get too close either.

There was more to Nick Rogers than he wanted her to know. And the more time she spent around him, the more convinced she was that he was hiding something from her.

ON THE RIDE HOME from the movie, Nick noticed that Laney seemed lost in thought.

"Did you enjoy the movie?" he asked, realizing he couldn't even recall the plot. He'd spent the time too aware of the woman sitting next to him.

"Yes. I'm just worried about my cousin," she said.

He wasn't sure he believed that. Laney had been distant since the park earlier. He feared it was something he'd said. Or hadn't.

"I've been wondering myself whether Geraldine left Maddie something out of gratitude for helping her from time to time—or to keep Maddie quiet," he said.

"What?"

He saw her shocked, angry expression and wondered why he'd brought this up. To get her take on it? Or to keep her at arms length?

"I'm just trying to understand their relationship and maybe what is going on with your cousin. Geraldine supposedly didn't have any enemies. Nor friends, from what I can tell. Maddie *was* one of the few people allowed in that house. I have to ask myself, why Maddie?"

"Because Maddie is sweet and nice and—"

"I didn't mean to upset you," Nick said looking over at her, wondering if that was true.

She turned away from him as if to look out the side window into the darkness.

"Did you notice how much Geraldine was paying Maddie?" he asked.

"Two dollars an hour," she said, "which proves that Maddie was helping her out of the goodness of her heart—not some dark ulterior motive."

"Or Maddie was getting a lot more than two bucks an hour so she wasn't about to ask for more."

Laney glared over at him. "You've spent time around Maddie. Do you really believe she's a blackmailer?"

He had to admit Maddie was the furthest thing from his image of a blackmailer. "But Maddie is all messed up, even you have to admit that or she wouldn't still want to marry Bo Evans."

"You won't get any argument out of me in that regard, but she wasn't blackmailing Geraldine Shaw."

"Someone apparently was. Which brings up the question of what Geraldine had to hide."

"Nothing."

He shook his head. "Most people have something to hide no matter how small."

She cocked a brow at him. "Like you?"

The question surprised him. Even in the dim light from the dash, he could see that she was serious. He'd thought he'd been so careful, but obviously he'd made her suspicious somehow. He grinned. "We all have our little secrets. Even you, I'd bet."

He saw something fleeting in her eyes. Laney was an open book. Or was she? Maybe it was true. Maybe everyone really did have things they wanted to hide.

He quickly changed the subject back to Geraldine. "You said her husband died last year?"

"At the end of the summer. Laci and I had already left when it happened."

Nick frowned. "I didn't see his grave up on the hill. In fact, the only grave near Geraldine's was an unnamed child."

"Geraldine lost her daughter a month before the baby was born." Laney's voice was flat. She seemed resigned to talking about Geraldine's murder rather than what he had to hide although she obviously wasn't happy about it.

"She never had any other children?"

Laney shook her head. "My grandmother said Geraldine never wanted *any* children. The baby had been Ollie's idea. There is some sort of birth defect that ran in Geraldine's family. I guess she feared it would affect her baby—and she was right."

Nick took that in, kicking himself for bringing this subject up in the first place. No wonder Laney was leery of him. He would come on to her, then pull away as if he didn't know what he wanted. That was just it. He knew what he wanted. Her. And under other circumstances...

"As for Ollie, her husband," Laney continued, "he was back in Minnesota visiting relatives when he died. His last wish was to be buried back there."

Nick chewed that over for a moment. "Doesn't it seem funny to you that Geraldine wouldn't want to be buried beside him?"

She shrugged. "She had more ties to Old Town Whitehorse than Ollie. The house belonged to her grandparents who homesteaded here. I guess she wanted to be where her roots were. All her relatives are buried up on the hill."

He drove down the long road that ended just past her house. He understood roots better than she might imagine.

"So your roots are in Texas?"

"No," he said too quickly, then shook his head. "I have no real roots."

"That's right, you said your family was in the military and you moved a lot."

He could feel her gaze on him, feel her trying to understand him. "You're lucky. Your roots are here. I envy you that, the kind of history you have here."

"We all make our own history," she said. "Few of the young people stay here anymore because there aren't enough decent-paying jobs. Life here is changing."

"That's too bad." He studied her face for a moment as they neared her house. "What about you? Do you think you will ever settle here?"

"My sister is determined to. At least that's what she says."

"What about you?"

"I do love it here and, being an accountant, I'm sure I could make a career here."

"But?"

She looked away, biting down on her lower lip before she said, "It would take the right man for me to stay."

Nick felt her words pierce his heart. That right man definitely wasn't Nick Rogers.

LANEY KNEW HE WASN'T GOING to kiss her. As he walked her to her door, she heard his radio in the patrol car squawk. He trotted back to the car. She listened as the dispatcher told him there'd been another attack outside a bar back in Whitehorse.

"You'd better go," she called to him. "Thank you for dinner and the movie. It was nice."

As she started to open the front door, she heard his boots on the porch steps. An instant later, he spun her around and into his arms. And the next thing she knew, he was kissing her.

And then he was gone, leaving her standing on the porch, wondering if she'd only dreamed the kiss. But even she couldn't have dreamed such a kiss. Or such a man.

Nick Rogers left her dazed and wanting more. And while her analytical mind didn't like the odds, her heart was willing to bet it all on him.

Chapter Ten

On a hunch the next morning, Nick e-mailed the department that handled births and deaths in Minnesota and inquired about an Oliver "Ollie" Raymond Shaw who had died last summer while on a visit from Montana.

They had no record of Ollie's death. Nor did Montana.

At the *Milk River Examiner,* Nick asked Glen Whitaker to see if Geraldine had run an obituary for her husband. Sure enough. The obit said Ollie had died in North Pond, Minnesota, almost a year ago to the day.

Glen made a copy of the obituary for him and asked, "Any leads on Geraldine's murder or that other case?"

Nick wished he could tell Glen that he'd found the person who'd beaten him up. He doubted Glen wanted to hear that Nick suspected it had been a woman with a baseball bat.

"Not yet," he said. "But you'll be the first to know when I do."

Back at his office, Nick contacted the state department of investigation in Minnesota only to be told there was no town by the name of North Pond. No funeral home by the name of the one Geraldine Shaw had said in the obit had handled the arrangements. No cemetery where Ollie Shaw was said to have been buried.

Oliver "Ollie" Raymond Shaw had been born in Minneapolis, but as far as Minnesota knew, Ollie hadn't died there. Nor in Montana.

Nick sat for a moment, taking it all in. He'd been around cops long before he'd became one. Maybe that was why he felt as if he'd been a cop for way too long. He'd seen too much. And yet as the pieces started falling together, the picture that started forming made him sick to his stomach. Sometimes he hated this job.

On impulse, he unlocked the bottom desk drawer and took out the cell phone as he'd done each day since he'd arrived in Montana. Only all the other times there'd been no message.

His heart began to pound, fear making his palms sweat as he turned on the phone and retrieved the message. He told himself he was prepared for the worst. A message telling him to get the hell out of Dodge because Keller had found him. But he'd always known that by the time he was sent that message, he'd probably already be dead.

Maybe that was why he'd feared the other message as well. The voice on the other end of the line was flat, official. The message was short and sweet.

"The trial's been moved up. We'll need you here by the beginning of next week."

A blade of ice wedged itself in his heart. He had to go back to California. He recoiled at the thought, but if he didn't return, he'd have more than Keller to worry about. As if Keller wasn't enough to cause him sleepless nights.

Next week.

A part of him wanted to run. But there was no place he'd ever be safe. He'd known that when he'd come to Montana. Not even out here in the Big Open would he ever be free of his past.

In the meantime, he had a murder on his hands. He picked up his car keys and headed for Old Town Whitehorse. At the edge of town, he spotted Chaz pulling a large red wagon, his dog walking beside it.

Nick pulled over when he saw the expression on Chaz's face.

"I guess you heard Prince got in trouble again," Chaz said quickly as Nick got out. "But I'm returning everything he borrowed."

"Borrowed?" Nick asked, looking into the wagon. It held a variety of items, everything from a garden sprinkler to a TV remote.

"Prince took all of this stuff from people's houses?" Nick asked, picking up an old baseball bat.

"He's really smart. He knows how to open screen doors." The boy's shoulders slumped. "He's been going into people's houses and taking things."

Nick stared down at the bat in his hands. The bat

was weathered and cracked. In one crack there was a dark red crusted substance that unless he missed his guess was blood.

"Where did Prince get this?" Nick asked, trying to keep his voice even.

Chaz shrugged. "I don't know where he got any of the stuff. I'm going from house to house and letting people take back the things that belong to them. And apologize for Prince like my aunt told me to."

Nick nodded, trying to decide how best to handle this. "This bat looks familiar. Will you do me a favor? Keep track of who takes what so I can write up a report. Don't make a big deal out of it. I don't want any of the residents to press charges against you. You think you can remember who takes what?"

Chaz nodded quickly.

Nick placed the bat back into the wagon. "After you return everything, write it all down and I'll stop by and pick it up, okay?"

"Yes, sir. And there won't be any more problems with Prince. My aunt says I have to keep him on a chain in the yard at night from now on."

"That's probably a good idea," Nick agreed before climbing back into his patrol car and driving up the road to Maddie Cavanaugh's.

LANEY STUMBLED ACROSS the Web site quite by accident. It was amateurishly done with lots of bells and whistles and bright colors.

She almost didn't click on the "Take a Tour" of prospective dates. But her curiosity got the better of her.

The first face that came up was no surprise. Violet. It was an awful photo, cropped down from a regular photograph into a mug shot. Poor Violet. Laney was sure the woman hadn't agreed to this photo, let alone being on the site.

The next prospective date was a woman who lived in Whitehorse. Laney couldn't remember her name, but she recognized her face. What was interesting about the photo was that Arlene had left some of the background in this one.

With a start, Laney realized that the photograph had been taken at the engagement party that Laci had thrown for Maddie and Bo.

"What's going on?" Laci asked, coming into the room. "Did I hear you swear?"

Laney hadn't realized she'd even spoken. "You aren't going to believe this," she said to her sister as she quickly clicked to the next photo.

"I know that woman. She was at the party," Laci said as she pulled up a chair.

"I suspect they were all at the party," Laney said as she advanced through the photographs until hers came up. Her mouth fell open—just as it was in the candid snapshot that Arlene Evans had taken of her at the engagement party.

"No," Laci said beside her. "She didn't."

Arlene had caught Laney in the middle of saying something. It was the least flattering photograph

Laney had ever seen of herself. But to make matters worse, Arlene had "coupled" Laney with Deputy Sheriff Nick Rogers as a "match." His photo was at least better than hers.

"I can't believe this," Laney said. "She put me up on her Web site without my knowledge?" And surely Nick hadn't signed up on Meet-a-Mate, had he?

Laci reached over and advanced to the next photograph. "At least she got one of me that isn't too bad, and look—you can see some of the desserts I made in the background."

"Wait a minute," Laney said as she stared at the photograph of her sister. "Arlene didn't take this one." The photograph had been shot down the table so even though Arlene had cropped out the people at the dessert table, she hadn't been able to get them completely out of the photograph.

"You're right," Laci said. "That's Arlene's hand there. I recognize her ring and that must be her daughter Charlotte's hand complete with fake fingernails."

"But whose hand is that?" Laney shivered. "That must be Geraldine's reaching for the last macaroon." She looked over at her sister. "I've got to tell Nick about this. If there's more of these photographs, there could be one of the killer putting the poison macaroon on the plate."

NICK FOUND MADDIE OUT behind her mother's house working in the flower garden. She seemed lost in a world of her own, oblivious to everything but the dark soil she was digging in.

"Hello, Maddie."

She started, surprise and instant fear in her eyes. "I didn't hear you drive up."

He'd purposely parked down the road and walked. The times he'd called, her mother had always told him her daughter wasn't home. Maddie had taken to parking her car behind the house or in the garage, so even the times he'd stopped by, Sarah Cavanaugh had covered for Maddie.

Nick had known he was getting a runaround. He could have pushed it, but he hadn't. As worried as he'd been about Maddie, he hadn't had an official reason to force a conversation. Until now.

"Did you used to help Geraldine with her gardening?" he asked as he took a seat on a small bench beside a bed of petunias.

"Sometimes," Maddie said looking nervous.

"I've never raised anything in a garden, but I'd like to try sometime."

She looked up at him. "Don't people have gardens in Houston?"

"Sure, the ones who live outside the city. I was a city kid though, all concrete and asphalt. My mother used to have this pot with cherry tomatoes in it that she kept in the window. That's about the closest I ever got to real dirt."

"That's sad," she said as she turned a clump of earth with her spade, loosening it, before digging up what must have been a weed because she tossed it into a pile she'd made behind her on the grass.

"What did Geraldine grow?" he asked.

"Why do you keep asking me about her?"

"I still have to find out who killed her," he said.

"But what she grew doesn't have anything to do with her being dead," Maddie said.

"Doesn't it?" he asked.

She stared down at her spade. "I don't know anything about it. I already told you that."

"Tell me this. A year ago this month, did you help her put in a new flower bed beside her house?"

She looked up in shock, her eyes wide.

"Who helped her with the body?" Nick asked.

"What?"

"Her husband's body. Geraldine wouldn't have been able to move the body by herself. I asked around. Ollie was a big man. She would have needed help. Your help since you were her friend. Her only close friend."

Maddie was shaking her head, her eyes full of tears. "He had a heart attack. She couldn't afford to have him buried."

"You know better than that. You helped her cover up what she'd done. Why?"

Maddie was crying now, sobbing as if a dam had broken. "She was nice to me. She was teaching me to crochet and cook and to grow flowers. She said I was like a daughter to her. She let me make messes. She never yelled at me if I didn't get it right."

He stared at the girl. "Didn't your own mother do that?"

"Mother hated it when I made a mess. She would shoo me outside. I would go to Geraldine's and she would…" She cried as if there was no end to her tears, no longer able to speak.

"Who did you tell about Ollie?" Nick asked when she'd caught her breath.

She glanced toward the house and made a swipe at her tears.

"It's just you and me," Nick said. He'd been relieved to see that Sarah's car was gone when he'd driven by the house before he'd parked down the road. "Maddie, whoever you told about what happened was blackmailing Geraldine. Was it Bo you told?"

She shook her head frantically.

"Geraldine was running out of money. I think she told her blackmailer that she wasn't going to pay him anymore. Maybe she even threatened to turn herself in—and him with her—so he killed her."

"I didn't tell *anyone*. I swear it." She glanced toward the house again.

"But someone figured it out, figured out that Geraldine killed Ollie?" he asked.

She was crying again, stabbing the spade into the ground as she spoke. "Ollie was sick. He didn't know what he was doing. She didn't mean to kill him, just stop him from hurting me."

Nick's eyes widened. "Oh, my God, Maddie." He

reached for her, drawing her to him as she sobbed in his arms. "It's all right. It's all right," he kept saying. But it was far from all right.

Everything was starting to make sense. The change Laney said she'd seen in her cousin after last summer. The way Maddie had let Bo and his family mistreat her. It all made a sick kind of sense. Anyone familiar with sexual-abuse victims would have recognized the symptoms sooner.

Maddie's sobs finally slowed, then shuddered to a stop.

"Geraldine killed him because he was hurting you," Nick said softly. "That's why you helped her bury his body." He pulled back to look in her eyes. "It wasn't your fault, Maddie. You have to know that."

She nodded, but he could see that she didn't really believe it.

"Who figured it out, Maddie? Who was blackmailing Geraldine?" Who had taken advantage of what had happened to this young woman and used it to extort money from the one person Maddie had loved and trusted?

Maddie looked toward the house again.

He felt her shudder and turned slowly, already knowing what he would see—Sarah Cavanaugh's face in the window.

"Your *mother?*"

LANEY WAS EXCITED WHEN SHE heard Nick's voice on the phone. She'd even been thinking about calling him. Maybe inviting him to dinner. Getting Laci to cook something special and disappear for the evening.

"Laney, I need your help," Nick said.

"Of course you do," she joked, then belatedly registered that he didn't sound like himself. She dropped into a chair at the kitchen table. "What's wrong?"

"It's Maddie. Can we come right over?"

"Of course," she said. "But, Nick, what—" She realized he'd hung up. She stood holding the receiver, her heart pounding so hard her chest hurt. Maddie. A thousand thoughts chased around in her head. But he'd said *we*. Can *we* come over? He had to mean him and Maddie. So it couldn't be that bad, right?

Unfortunately, as she went to wait on the porch, Laney kept hearing the tone of Nick's voice. Something was terribly wrong. She stood at the railing watching the road as she'd done her first day here this summer, only this time, she *knew* it would be bad news.

Maddie looked a mess when she got out of the patrol car. Laney could see that she'd been crying. Her face was puffy and red, her eyes downcast.

Laney ran to her and threw her arms around her cousin. Bo Evans. That was what it had to be about. What had that man done now? It didn't matter. Whatever it was, they would deal with it. She would deal with it. As she held her cousin, she watched Nick get out of the car. He looked devastated.

"I'm getting you dirty. I was planting flowers," Maddie said as she pulled back to look down at her dirty gardening clothes and the soil on her hands. Tears welled in her eyes. "Can I get a shower?"

"Just a minute," Nick said. He went into the house, leaving them alone.

"What's wrong, Maddie?" Laney asked.

But her cousin only shook her head. "I just need a shower. And some clothes. I need some clothes."

"Of course." The monotone of her cousin's voice was enough to scare Laney. Something horrible had happened. But what?

Nick came out of the house and nodded to Maddie. She went inside, her movements like those of a sleepwalker as her shoes scuffed across the porch.

"What happened?" Laney demanded in a whisper the moment Maddie was out of earshot.

He raised a finger, stepped in the house and returned a few moments later. "I can hear the water running. I think she's in the shower. I removed anything she could hurt herself with from the bathrooms."

Laney felt her eyes widen, then tear as she swallowed back the lump in her throat. "Why would she hurt herself?"

"I think you'd better sit down."

He didn't have to tell her twice. She dropped into the chair on the porch, the day's heat making waves across the dark soil of the road, a faint breeze carrying the scent of hay and dust and inevitably the end of summer. The end of a lot of things.

Laney would never forget that moment or the way Nick drew his chair up next to hers and cupped her hands in his and softly said the words that shattered her heart.

NICK HELD LANEY IN HIS ARMS. He could feel her pain, her anger. He was having trouble dealing with his own. Sometimes he hated being a cop. He'd thought he'd escaped it up here in Montana. But human nature could be ugly and geography didn't change that.

At the sound of water shutting off inside the house, Laney hurriedly dried her eyes and pulled back from him.

"I need to see to my cousin," she said. "What about Aunt Sarah?"

"She's agreed to turn herself in."

"Does Uncle Roy know?" Laney asked.

Nick nodded. "He didn't take it well."

"No, I'm sure he didn't. Thank you. I knew something was wrong, but I had no idea."

"None of us did," Nick said. "She needs counseling."

Laney nodded. "Don't worry. I'll see that she gets whatever she needs."

"I knew you would." He rose. "I'll call you."

Laney nodded as she opened the screen door and stepped inside the house.

Nick moved through the afternoon heat to his car. He rolled down the windows as he drove slowly back toward Whitehorse. He felt sick to his stomach. He was just thankful that Maddie had Laney and Laci in her life.

Not far down the road, he saw Chaz coming down the road pulling his wagon along the edge of the barren pit. Prince trotted beside the boy, his tongue lolling. The day had gotten fierce and even now with the sun dipping toward the western horizon, the heat still beared down oppressively.

Nick slowed the car as he came alongside the boy. "How did it go?" he asked, glancing toward the wagon.

"No one claimed the bat," Chaz said, sounding apologetic. "I asked everyone. I don't know where Prince got it."

Possibly not from anyone's house. Someone could have thrown the bat away. The dog could have gotten it from anywhere.

"Did you make that list for me?" Nick asked.

"Yes, sir." He dug a stubby piece of pencil from his pocket, then a wadded-up scrap of paper. "Sorry, it's kind of messy. But I printed real neat so you could read it."

Nick smiled. "You did a great job." He glanced at the list, then put it on the seat next to him. "Would you mind if I took the bat to see if I can find its owner?"

Chaz shook his head, clearly relieved since everything else had been accounted for, and handed Nick the baseball bat.

"In the meantime—"

"I'm going to keep Prince at home," the boy said with a grin.

"Good thinking," Nick said. "You might stay close to home as well." He told himself that the dog had probably found the baseball bat in a ditch or a trash can. If, as Nick suspected, the stain on the bat was blood, then the owner wouldn't have kept the weapon in his house, he would have disposed of it.

But as Nick drove back to Whitehorse, he couldn't help worrying as he glanced back to see the silhouette of the boy and his dog before both disappeared from view.

Chapter Eleven

"Maddie has agreed to get counseling," Laney said when Nick answered the phone Saturday. She couldn't believe how good it was to hear his voice. She hadn't seen him since he'd brought her the horrible news about Maddie. "Laci went with her to Billings."

"I'm glad. And Bo?"

"The deal Laci made with Maddie was that Bo wouldn't know where she was."

"Good," he said.

"So, you're staying for a while longer? Your grandfather told me you usually only stay a couple of weeks in the summer."

He sounded worried. Did he think she was staying because of him?

"Don't worry, I have to get back to work soon. But I can't leave until I'm sure that Maddie is all right." And until Geraldine's murderer was caught. Unless she already had been, Laney thought, thinking of her aunt Sarah.

Laney couldn't stand to think of what her aunt had done. "I can't believe Aunt Sarah didn't get Maddie help. And to use what she knew to bleed Geraldine dry..." She shook her head.

"Sarah was like everyone else. She apparently believed Geraldine was rich and wouldn't miss the money. At least that's her story," Nick said.

Laney sighed in disgust. "Do you think Geraldine knew that the person blackmailing her was Maddie's own mother?"

"I don't think she had any idea."

Laney braced herself and asked, "Did Aunt Sarah kill Geraldine?"

"She swears she didn't."

"You believe her?"

"There's no proof that she did. It will be up to the county attorney to decide what to charge her with. Sarah was smart enough not to put the money in her account, but she has admitted to blackmailing Geraldine."

"My uncle Roy is divorcing her," Laney said. "I've heard he's putting the place up for sale. He can't forgive Aunt Sarah and he's just so ashamed. I know how he feels, but a part of me is sorry for her. I think she thought marrying a Cavanaugh was a bigger deal than it was. Maddie told me that her mother felt she wasn't good enough for the rest of the family, that they looked down on her."

"Yeah, as a matter of fact I'm very familiar with *that* feeling in my own family," Nick quipped.

This was more like the Nick Rogers she'd come to know. Not the one who'd sounded so businesslike on the phone just moments before. She chewed at her lip for a moment. "I've missed you."

Silence.

Then a sigh. "I've missed you, too. Laney—"

"I was thinking you might come out for dinner tonight. I'm not as good a cook as my sister, but I try."

More silence. She could hear her pulse pounding in her ears, her heart a drum inside her chest. What was it about this man? Why did it matter so much? She didn't know. She just knew it did matter.

"I can't tonight, but thanks for the offer."

"Okay, how about tomorrow night then?" she asked, shocked by her own boldness.

She heard him shuffle his feet, move something on his desk, and grimaced. "Are you sure about this, Laney?"

Yes. No. "I'll be going back to Arizona Monday." She almost added that she had stumbled across something that might help solve Geraldine's murder, but she hated that she'd resorted to even telling him she was leaving to get him to come over for dinner. And she wasn't sure Arlene even had the photos in her camera anymore.

"What time?" he said, sounding resigned.

"How does seven sound?" she asked, more excited than she'd been in too long to remember.

"Seven. Fine. What can I bring?"

"Just your appetite," she said and wanted to bite her tongue.

A beat of silence when she knew they were both thinking about a completely different kind of appetite that had nothing to do with food.

"I'll see you at seven."

She hung up before he would change his mind. She'd heard his fear. Had he been hurt in a relationship? Was that why he was so afraid of where this was going between the two of them?

Or was he just afraid of being alone with her?

Well, tomorrow night he wouldn't have a choice. It would just be the two of them, alone on a warm summer night. For the last time.

NICK MENTALLY KICKED HIMSELF for accepting Laney's invitation. He'd promised himself he'd keep his distance. Especially since he'd be leaving as well. Right after dinner. Right after he said goodbye to Laney.

It had felt like a death sentence. Hell, it could very well be one if Keller got word he'd returned to the state of California.

He was glad Laney was going back to Arizona. Mesa wasn't that far from L.A. Depending on how things went, maybe… He shoved that thought away. He couldn't let himself go down that road. Even if things went well in California, he wasn't sure she'd want to see him once she knew who he really was.

For so long it had only been about staying hidden, staying alive. Laney had made him forget all that. She'd made him hopeful. She'd made him want not only her, but also a life. He knew that even if Keller didn't kill him first, he wouldn't have a life after the trial.

He looked at the list in his hand. Chaz had written down all the items he'd returned—and to which houses.

Nick had overnighted the baseball bat to the crime lab in Missoula along with DNA samples from each of the men who'd been attacked. He'd seen enough weapons with dried blood on them. All he needed was verification that the blood was human. And if he could get a DNA match....

When the phone rang, he jumped.

"Deputy Sheriff Rogers," he answered, surprised how easily he'd been able to play this role. Maybe it had been the years he'd spent undercover, pretending he was someone he wasn't. Right now this role felt more real than his old life in California.

"This is Maximilian Roswell with the crime lab." Nick held his breath.

"That bat you sent us? Just as you suspected, the substance on it is definitely human blood."

"Were you able to get a DNA sample from it?"

"As a matter of fact, it matched up with one of the other samples you sent us. A Curtis McAlheney's."

McAlheney's nose had bled, splattering all over

he'd said. Nick let out the breath he'd been holding and got off the line as quickly as possible. He called Chaz's house, spoke with the boy's aunt. Chaz and Prince were just outside in the yard, she assured him.

"Please make sure they stay there," Nick said.

"Is that dog in trouble again?" the aunt asked, sounding more weary than upset.

"Not at all," Nick said. "That's a very smart dog. He might have just helped me solve one of my cases."

Nick hung up and picked up his keys. What worried him was that one of those residents had recognized the bat but hadn't claimed it, afraid of incriminating himself.

Nick couldn't have the assailant thinking Chaz still had that bat. The last thing he wanted to do was put the kid in danger, although Prince had already done that with his thieving.

At the hardware store, Nick bought a baseball bat like the one the dog had stolen and a small can of dark reddish-brown paint. He took it back to his apartment, roughed up the bat on his concrete back step, then taking a rag he added just enough of the paint until the bat looked like the old one he'd gotten from Chaz.

Tossing the bat into his patrol car, he headed for Whitehorse. As he drove, he went over the list in his head that Chaz had made him. There was one house in that neighborhood that apparently the dog hadn't taken anything from. At least, no one at that house had claimed any of the items.

And yet Nick knew for a fact that the dog had been in that house.

LANEY WAS TOO RESTLESS to hang around home. The place felt empty without Laci there. Laney had gotten a call that morning from her sister. Laci thought Maddie seemed to be doing better. The counseling was helping.

"Just a minute," Laci had said. "Maddie wants to say hello."

Maddie wanted to know if Bo had called. He hadn't.

"I'm going over to the Evanses' now as a matter of fact," Laney had told her. "Is there a message you want me to give him?"

"No. That's okay."

Laney felt for her cousin. All she could do was hope that the counseling would make Maddie see what kind of man Bo Evans really was.

As Laney neared the Evanses' house, she saw the ambulance pulling away, lights flashing. She pulled to the side of the road to let it pass, then hurriedly drove down to the house to see what had happened.

Violet answered the door looking as if she'd just woken up. She wore a muumuu, the fabric faded and worn, and fuzzy pink bunny slippers.

"I saw the ambulance," Laney said.

Violet nodded. "Mother took too many of her pain pills."

"Is she all right?" Laney asked.

"They pumped her stomach, but they wanted to take her to the hospital for observation."

Laney stared at the woman. "They think she might have taken the pills on purpose?"

Bo came into the room from down the hall. He, too, looked as if he'd just gotten up although it was after eleven. He was wearing a wrinkled T-shirt and pajama bottoms, his feet bare.

"What are you telling her?" he demanded of his sister. "Mom didn't try to kill herself. It was an accident. Her broken arm's been bothering her. She just got confused about how many pills she'd taken."

He gave Violet a dirty look as he turned and went into the kitchen.

Violet looked after him, no love in her gaze.

Laney wondered where Charlotte was, then remembered she hadn't seen her car. The only one of the Evans offspring with a job, Charlotte must be at work. Charlotte was the shampoo girl at the Clip and Curl. She also was learning to do nails, Laney had heard.

"Well, I'm sorry to hear about your mother," Laney said. More sorry than she wanted to admit. She'd hoped to talk to Arlene. She'd especially wanted Arlene to take the Laney and Nick "match" photo off her Web site. But she also had hoped to get copies of the photographs from the party to show to Nick.

In the kitchen, Bo was banging pots and pans as if searching for something.

"Your mother was going to give me copies of the photographs she took at Maddie's and Bo's party," she fibbed to Violet. "I would be happy to pay for them."

Violet looked at her as if she'd lost her mind. "Geraldine dropped dead at that party."

"Yes, I remember," Laney said. "I promised your mother twenty for the copies but I'll pay more if—"

Before Violet could answer, Bo came out. "How much more?" he demanded.

"Forty dollars," Laney said, wincing at the greed she saw shining in his eyes.

"I don't know why you'd want photographs from *that* party, the party from hell, but I can make you copies."

Laney stood in the living room, Violet waiting as well. Neither spoke. Laney could hear Bo in a back room mumbling to himself as a printer whirred. At one point, she thought about sitting down, eyed the plastic-covered furniture and decided to remain standing.

When Bo came out with a couple dozen photographs, she gave him two twenty-dollar bills from her purse. He took them, stuffed it in his pocket and went back into the kitchen without a word.

Laney let herself out.

NICK PASSED THE AMBULANCE on the way to Old Town. He got on his radio and found out that Arlene Evans had overdosed on drugs and was being taken to the hospital. Turning around, he followed the ambulance back into Whitehorse.

Arlene was conscious, sitting up in bed, complaining to the nurse when he entered her room.

"How are you doing?" he asked her.

"I'm fine," she snapped. "I don't know why everyone is making such a fuss. I mixed up my pills. It could have happened to anyone."

"I was on my way out to your house when I saw the ambulance," Nick said. "I just wanted to check on you."

Arlene softened a little. "That was nice of you. But it doesn't make up for you arresting my son for something he didn't do."

Whatever. "Well, I can see that you're going to be fine." He started to turn from her bed to leave, when he caught a whiff of her perfume.

"What?" she demanded, no doubt seeing the look on his face.

"Your perfume. It's familiar."

"You like it?" she asked, smiling broadly. "It was my mother's. I get compliments on it all the time. It's my favorite. It reminds me of my mother. She loved lavender."

ON THE WAY OUT TO THE EVANS house, Nick debated what he was about to do. It was a gamble. A risk he wasn't sure he should take. But it was Saturday afternoon. And he was determined to tie up some loose ends before he left.

He thought about Laney, about saying goodbye. He would do that tomorrow night. She wouldn't know it was goodbye though.

The thought that he would probably never see her again devastated him. He'd considered canceling dinner, knowing seeing her again would only make it that much harder to say goodbye. Selfishly he wanted that last evening with her.

Just as he had to take this gamble tonight, he thought, as he parked in front of the Evans house, and taking the baseball bat, climbed out, noting that all three Evans offspring appeared to be home since it was still early evening.

In the distance, Nick could make out a tractor in a field, the silhouette of a man hunched over the wheel, the tractor dragging something that stirred up dust as the driver inched across the horizon.

At his knock, Violet peered at Nick through the screen. In the background, he could hear loud music and Bo's souped-up car was parked out front.

"I was hoping your mother was home," Nick said, lying through his teeth.

"She's at the hospital," Violet said.

"I hope it's nothing serious."

"No." She glanced from Nick to the bat at his side.

"Mind if I come in?" he asked, raising his voice.

Without a word, she pushed open the screen door and motioned him inside. He noticed she was wearing what looked like the dresses his great-aunt wore. On Violet's feet were furry bunny slippers.

Past her on the plastic couch was Charlotte. She was wearing a crop top and short shorts. She had her legs tucked under herself and she was chewing on the end of a lock of her hair as she watched something on television.

"Did you want to see Bo?" Violet asked.

Nick noted that the music had stopped. "I thought one of you could help me. That new boy in the neighborhood has a dog that picks up things," he said over the sound of the television. Loud enough that Bo would be able to hear down the hall. "I thought this might belong to one of you." He held up the bat.

As expected, Bo's curiosity was peaked at what Nick was offering. He came out of his room and down the hall, looking disheveled and half-asleep.

"Where the hell did you get my old bat?" he demanded.

"This is *yours?*" Nick asked.

Bo held out a hand. Nick slapped the bat into Bo's palm. "Hell, yes, it's mine. I wondered what happened to it."

"Has it been missing long?" Nick asked.

"Long enough," Bo said. "How did some dog get it?"

Nick shrugged. "I wasn't even sure it was yours.

The boy brought it around. I thought he showed it to you and you said it wasn't yours."

Bo shot a look at Violet. "Did some kid bring this bat by here and you told him it wasn't mine?"

"How was I to know it was your bat?" Violet demanded. "Charlotte said yours got broken."

Bo swung around to glare at his youngest sister.

"I said I thought it had." Charlotte shrugged. "It's old and icky, why do you want it anyway?"

Bo was shaking his head and swinging the bat, clearly angry.

"Well, you have it back now," Nick said and turned to leave, glancing at Charlotte. She had stopped chewing on her hair. She dragged her gaze away from the television. He saw the tension in her expression. Was she worried that he was going to tell Bo that she was the one who'd let the dog into the house? She swung her gaze back at the television.

"Tell your mother I stopped by," Nick said.

"You tell that kid to keep his damn dog away from my house!" Bo called as Nick walked out to his patrol car and climbed in. He was shaking inside. Partly from fear he'd just messed up big-time. And partly from the bad vibes he'd felt inside the house. Add to that the faint hint of lavender and it had the makings of a deadly potion.

THERE WAS ONLY ONE LIVE BAND in town Saturday night at one of the four bars.

Nick staked out the bar with the band, finding

himself a place where he could watch the back of the building without being seen.

The night was cool and very dark, and he was counting on the person with the bat making an appearance. Unless the assailant realized Nick had returned the wrong bat. Or unless Nick had taken the bat to the wrong house.

There were too many variables. Too much chance that he was way off base.

He tried not to second-guess himself as the hours went by. He knew that the men who'd been attacked had all left by the back door of the bar before closing. He was betting they had followed someone out. Or had been lured out.

He tried to concentrate on the back door, on who would come through it before the night was over. But his mind kept going to Laney and dinner tomorrow night.

Then he would be gone. He already had a story ready to tell the sheriff's department. He would be returning home to take care of a sick relative.

Just returning to the state of California would be dangerous. Standing up in court to testify against Zak Keller would be a death warrant. That was if he even made it as far as the courtroom. Keller had friends who would die to protect him—and the truth from coming out.

No, Nick thought with a rueful smile, his life wasn't worth squat. Even a bookie wouldn't take odds on him coming out of this alive. But if he didn't testify, then Keller would go free. And if that happened, Nick was one dead SOB. Keller would hunt him down like a rabid dog even if it took the rest of his life.

His cell phone vibrated in his pocket. He swore under his breath as he heard the back door of the bar open. Music spilled out, a lot of bass guitar and drums. The phone vibrated again. The door closed with a swish, taking the music with it.

Just before the door shut, he saw the woman in the light spilling out. She wore a blue dress. He watched her walk to her car. She hesitated, standing in the darkness as if listening before she opened her car door.

His cell phone quit vibrating. He waited, afraid to breathe as she slid behind the wheel. She didn't start the car. Instead, she seemed to be watching the back door of the bar as if expecting someone.

Minutes ticked by. He saw her lean her head on the steering wheel. He could almost feel her disappointment, her heartbreak, as he watched Violet Evans finally start her car and pull away.

Nick swore under his breath. He'd been so sure that tonight was the night. And he'd had his money on Violet. The woman seemed to have no luck with men and her mother was always trying to push her off on some poor soul.

He could see where Violet might have a bad attitude when it came to men. She might take some pleasure in beating the crap out of them with a baseball bat after they'd disappointed her.

But he'd been wrong. Not about the bat belonging in that house; he'd been sure of it. Nick just didn't believe Bo had been the one using the bat. Nick could see Arlene Evans beating up men. Except, tonight she was in the hospital. Maybe that was why nothing was happening here.

Nick swore again. His patrol car was parked a few blocks over. He turned to leave when the back door of the bar opened again. He quickly melted back into the shadows.

A man stuck his head out, looked around, hesitating as if checking to make sure the coast was clear. He stepped out tentatively, glancing around, hitched up his pants and started toward an old brown pickup parked at the far end of the lot.

The darkness was complete. Nick couldn't put a name to the man, but he suspected it was the one Violet had been waiting for. The man who'd stood her up.

Just as the man neared his pickup, Nick spotted movement coming out of the dark alley. The figure came up fast behind the man. Nick didn't even see the swing of the bat, but he heard the sound of it as the bat connected with the man's back. The man let out an *ufft* sound and sprawled facedown in the dirt. The figure, wearing a black hooded cloak, moved quickly toward the man.

"What the hell." Nick was running, his weapon drawn. He covered the distance between him and the scene at a sprint.

The dark figure wound up for another whack with the bat. Nick grabbed the bat and wrenched it free, shoving the barrel end of the pistol into the back of the assailant as he yelled, "Police! Freeze!"

Nick dropped the bat and reached for his flashlight. He'd recognized the black cloak. It was just like the one Violet had worn at Geraldine Shaw's funeral. He jerked the hood down and, stepping around, shoved the light into the woman's face.

Charlotte Evans blinked blindly. He lowered the beam to the ground in shock.

Charlotte focused her gaze on him and smiled. "I had a feeling that I shouldn't come into town tonight."

IT WAS THE WEE HOURS of morning by the time Nick got Charlotte Evans booked and locked up.

He'd read her her rights, warning her not to say anything she would regret.

"I don't regret anything," she said. "They all deserved it." She saw that he didn't get it. "Men like that." She shook her head. "They are nice to me because I'm pretty." Her expression turned sour. "But I hated the way they were with my sister. They thought they could treat her any way they wanted just because she isn't pretty. That's not right. Someone needed to do something."

He had to call her mother, wake Arlene up at the hospital and get cussed out for arresting her daughter. Nick doubted Charlotte would spend more than a night in jail. He knew she would never get to trial.

First off, the assaulted men wouldn't press charges. Not against a seventeen-year-old girl. Especially not after word got out why she'd done what she had. Charlotte Evans would skate.

But Nick had a bad feeling that it wouldn't be the last the people of Montana heard of Charlotte Evans. He'd seen the way she'd swung that bat. It gave him chills to think she'd be out on the street again.

It wasn't until the next morning, after a fitful night with bad dreams and little sleep, that Nick remembered the call he'd gotten while staking out the bar.

He checked the message. It was from the crime lab.

He returned the call to Maximilian Roswell's cell.

"I just got your message," Nick said, apologizing for calling on a Sunday.

"Thought you'd want to know that we narrowed down the chemical compound found in the poison that killed Geraldine Shaw," Maximilian said. "The compound has been off the market for quite a while now, but I can tell you what it was used for anyway. Artificial-nail remover."

Nick blinked. "What?"

"You heard me right. This particular brand had enough cyanide in it to kill."

Nick rubbed his forehead with his fingers. Arlene Evans had artificial nails. So did Charlotte, her daughter. And so did Sarah Cavanaugh, he recalled with a start. And Sarah Cavanaugh had a motive for killing Geraldine.

The dispatcher appeared in his door, motioning that he had an urgent call.

"I'm going to have to get back to you on this," Nick said and got off the line.

"It's the hospital. Someone just tried to smother Arlene Evans with a pillow. The person got away. The deputy on call is searching the area but so far nothing."

As Nick left his office, he heard the cell phone in his bottom drawer ring, but he didn't turn back. He didn't want to know that the trial had been postponed. Laney was leaving Monday. Nick just wanted it over.

Nick didn't answer the phone. It quit ringing as he drove away. He didn't hear the man on the other end of the line leave a short, succinct message: "Your cover is blown. Get out now."

Chapter Twelve

Laney called her sister Sunday morning to ask Laci what she should make for dinner.

"Something exotic. Something he's never had before." Laci started rattling off dishes Laney had never even heard of and she realized it had been a mistake asking her sister what to cook.

"I think I should keep it simple. Make something homey like meat loaf and mashed potatoes and fresh peas from the garden. Maybe a carrot-and-raisin salad."

"You've got to be kidding," Laci cried. "You need to wow him with your culinary capacities."

Laney would rather wow him with her intelligence, her sense of humor, her native charm. On second thought, maybe she *should* cook something exotic.

"How's Maddie?" she asked.

"Doing a lot better. The therapist let her call Bo. He broke off the engagement. He said she was nothing but trouble and blamed her for everything. The therapist listened in on the call. After Maddie hung up, she was upset and hurt, but seemed to finally see Bo Evans for the kind of man he is."

"That's good. I hope Maddie means it."

"Enjoy your dinner with Nick. I can't believe how well you two fit together," Laci gushed.

Laney laughed. "It's just a summer fling. I'm leaving Monday to go home." She hoped neither of those statements proved true. "Have you changed your mind about staying in Montana and starting your catering business here?"

"No. But I hate the thought that I won't see you until Thanksgiving."

"Who said I was coming back to Whitehorse for Thanksgiving?" Laney asked smiling, knowing her sister only too well.

"Of course you'll be back. You'll want to see Nick."

That much was true. She *would* want to see Nick, she thought as she hung up. For the first summer in all the years she'd been coming here, Laney didn't want to leave. She'd extended her time here as long as she could unless she was her own boss.

She concentrated on what to cook. She wanted dinner to be comfortable. Maybe she'd regret it, but she was going with meat loaf. That decided, she set about getting things ready.

What to wear was much harder. Neither with her clothing nor her cooking did she want to appear too anxious, let alone desperate. Once the meat loaf was in the oven, the potatoes boiling on the stove, the peas picked and shelled and ready to be cooked, she would get dressed. She didn't want to be rushing around when he arrived.

When the time came, she decided on her favorite sundress, pulled her hair up into a ponytail and dabbed on just a touch of lip gloss. Understated.

That was her.

She had the table set on the porch, one lantern candle at the center. She hadn't even used the good china, although she was debating going back in for it when she heard the sound of a car coming up the road.

Her heart began to pound, her palms sweat, her mouth going dry at the sight of Nick Rogers as he got out of the patrol car. He wore jeans, a button-down long-sleeved shirt and boots. He looked shy and scared and happy to see her.

She smiled down at him from the porch. "Tell me you like meat loaf."

He grinned. "I *love* meat loaf."

Laney laughed. "How about a beer before dinner?"

"You really *are* a woman after my own heart," he said as he bounded up the steps to join her on the porch. He was so close she could smell the clean masculine scent of him. She breathed him in as if taking her last breath.

He stood so closely, his look so intimate, she felt a bolt of desire shoot through her. "I can get the beer," he said softly.

She could only nod, watching him go through the door into the house before she grabbed the back of a chair to steady herself. Her nipples were as hard as pebbles and pressed tight against her silk bra—and the thin material of the dress. She felt flushed. She wanted to skip dinner altogether. She wanted him to take her here on the porch in front of everyone who happened by.

She jumped at his touch.

"You look hot," he said next to her ear.

And the next thing she knew, he was pressing the icy sweating bottle of beer to her temple.

"How's that?" he asked softly.

She didn't dare look at him for fear he would see her answer, know her heart, cause the Old Town Whitehorse gossip hotline to burn for weeks with talk of her and Nick Rogers and what happened on her front porch—and on a Sunday.

"Laney." He pressed one of the beers into her hand and met her gaze. "Laney," he said again.

Her gaze locked with his.

If he didn't kiss her, she knew she would scream. She ached for his touch, her breasts heavy, her nipples as hard as she was soft inside.

Without breaking contact with her gaze, he took her beer from her and touched the cold, wet bottle to her hard nipple through the cloth. She closed her eyes, a soft moan escaping her lips.

Putting both bottles on the table, he circled her waist with one arm and dragged her to him. She felt the heat of his mouth, of his body, the cold wet of his hand on her breast, then snaking up her thighs, under her panties to her center.

She let out a moan of pleasure, throwing her head back, as he dropped his mouth to her breast. She'd never wanted a man the way she wanted him. Never dreamed she could feel such intensity, such desire. She'd always been careful with her heart.

But as Nick swept her up, she wrapped her arms around his neck and kissed him with a need that felt fatal if not fulfilled. The ache inside her was heart deep.

He kicked open the screen door and took her inside where it was cool and dim and the neighbors wouldn't see her surrender to him.

In a fever, she pulled him to her, her mouth hot on his, her hands working at the buttons on his shirt, then the buttons on his jeans as he slipped the dress over her head.

She heard his intake of breath as his gaze moved like warm honey over her body, then his fingertips followed that same path. He shoved aside one bra strap, then the other. His mouth trailed from her lips down her throat to the crest of her breasts. She leaned back, her palms against the bare warm skin of his chest.

He took one nipple in his mouth, lathed it with his tongue, then the other. She groaned and pulled him closer; her hands dropped to his hips. She could feel his need, hard against her.

"Laney," he whispered as she drew him to the floor. "Laney."

The first time was fast and furious. She cried out, shuddering against him, their bodies damp and hot, their breathing coming hard and fast.

Later, lying in his arms, she barely heard the timer go off on the meat loaf. His stomach growled next to her and she laughed as she rolled over to prop herself up on one elbow and look down at him. She thought her heart would break at the tenderness in his gaze.

After the meat loaf, mashed potatoes and peas on the porch, when the sun had dissolved into the horizon and the air cooled, he turned out the light and made love to her on the porch.

She couldn't see his eyes in the darkness, but she could feel him. He made love to her as if memorizing every inch of her. As if this night would be his last.

"OH, MY GOD!" GLASS SHATTERED with a loud crash.

Nick bolted upright in bed at Laney's cry and the sound of breaking glass. He grabbed his gun from his holster on the floor by the bed and raced into the kitchen to find her standing in front of the television, what was left of a pitcher in pieces at her feet and orange juice swimming on the tile.

Wordlessly she pointed at the television.

He turned in time to see the face on the screen. A candid shot of him. It was there only a heart-seizing instant before it was replaced with a shot of

Arlene Evans sitting up in her hospital bed smiling into the camera.

"Well," Arlene was saying. "I came up with the idea to help young rural people. When you live in the part of Montana that we do, houses are miles apart. Towns are even farther apart. Not only do our young people have a lot of chores on the farms and ranches and not much time to date, they often don't get the opportunity to meet people their own ages. That's how I came up with Rural Montana Meet-a-Mate Internet dating service."

"No," Nick said as he laid his weapon on the kitchen counter. He couldn't believe this.

"She took photos of everyone at Maddie's and Bo's party and put them up on her site," Laney said. "But now we're all on national television."

National television. He was just as good as dead.

"I meant to tell you about this last night...." Laney let her words die off.

"You knew?" he snapped.

She froze, her expression clearly surprised and hurt by his tone, then started to take a step back.

"Don't move!" Her feet were bare and there were shards and orange juice everywhere. He grabbed the paper towels and bent down to pick up the broken pieces. "I'm sorry. It's just that..." It was just that he was screwed.

"I'm sorry, but there's glass all over," he said, trying to calm down. Seeing himself on TV had sent him into a tailspin.

"I was going to tell you and then I forgot," she said as he finished cleaning up the mess and tossed the paper towels and broken glass in the trash. "I went over to Arlene's and got copies of the photographs she'd taken at the party. I was going to show them to you because I thought there might be some evidence…"

He looked at her. She was wearing a silk robe that hugged the body he now knew by heart. Just looking at her made him ache for her.

Last night after she'd fallen asleep, he'd stared at her for a long time, desperately wanting her. And not just for a night. He'd never felt this way about a woman. It scared the hell out of him. Not just because his life wasn't his own right now. Not just because he could easily be dead tomorrow.

It scared him because he wanted Laney Cavanaugh tonight, tomorrow night and the next night for the rest of his life. He wanted to buy her a ring, ask her to marry him, stand at the altar and promise her his love forever.

He knew this was the real thing. He was in love with this woman. He reached for her, pulling her into his arms, holding her tight. He could feel her fear, her confusion. He cursed himself for letting this happen.

"I'm sorry. I have to go," he said and stepped back to take his gun off the counter, then hesitated as he looked at her. He opened his mouth, desperately needing to tell her the truth about everything, and closed it. He had to get out of Dodge. Now. "I'll call you later," he said as he headed for the bedroom.

"I have the photographs if you want—"

"It's too late for photographs," he said as he dressed. He looked up to find her standing in the bedroom doorway.

"What is it?" she asked, her eyes narrowing. "If it's about last night—"

"It's not." He stopped dressing. "Laney, last night was…unbelievable. I've never…" Words defied him. "But it shouldn't have happened. I can't get involved with anyone right now."

Her expression turned from hurt to anger. "You don't have to explain. I get it." She walked over to the bed and dropped the photographs on the comforter, then she turned and left.

He had to bite his tongue not to call her back. *Tell her, dammit. Just tell her the truth.* He swore as he strapped on his weapon. His photo was on national television. It wouldn't take Keller any time to find him. He had to get out of town. The best thing he could do for Laney was to distance himself from her and quickly.

He started to leave the photographs on the bed where she'd tossed them. But at the last minute, he scooped them up, planning to give them to one of the deputies in the department—once he'd destroyed all traces of ones with him in them. He didn't want any trail that would lead Keller to Laney in case things went badly in California.

At the front door, he stopped to look back toward the kitchen. The very last thing he wanted was to walk out this door. To walk out on Laney. But his life wasn't worth two cents right now. He had nothing to offer her. Absolutely nothing. Being around him would only put her in danger.

He opened the door and hurried across the porch, down the steps to his patrol car. He didn't look back. He couldn't.

LANEY WENT TO THE WINDOW to watch Nick go. To watch him run away. Last night had been just as he'd said—incredible. They'd been so close. Too close, she saw now. She knew he'd been afraid to let her into his life. She'd warned herself not to care too much.

Look at how he'd reacted to seeing his photograph on the Montana Meet-a-Mate site. Imagine how he would have reacted if he'd seen the two of them "matched-up" on the Web site. She could have killed Arlene for doing this. But she knew it wasn't Arlene's fault. Laney had known Nick wasn't ready to get involved with anyone. Maybe especially her.

There'd been sparks that first time she'd laid eyes on him. She wasn't sure when she'd fallen for him but she had. And now her heart was breaking.

She wanted to regret falling for Nick. To curse herself for last night. But she couldn't. She would have felt much worse if she'd left town without making love with him. The memory would haunt her always, but at least she had that.

The phone rang. Laney couldn't help the way her pulse surged as she reached to pick it up. *Let it be Nick. Please let it be Nick.*

"So?" Laci said. "Is he still there?"

"No," Laney said, trying to hide her disappointment on both counts. "He had to leave."

"Last night? Or this morning?"

Laney couldn't help smiling. "This morning."

"So?"

"It was wonderful. I'll never forget it. I was going to call you. I've decided to leave today rather than wait until tomorrow and drive to Billings to catch the plane."

"Wait a minute," Laci said. "You're leaving? What about Nick? Oh no, you made meat loaf, didn't you?"

"He loved the meat loaf. It was only a summer fling. Just like I told you."

"Why don't I believe that?" Laci asked.

"Because you are an incurable romantic. Listen, I have to get going. I'll call you when I get to Mesa. Give my love to Maddie."

"I'm sorry, Laney," her sister said before she could get off the phone.

NICK PLANNED HIS GETAWAY on the way back to Whitehorse. He had to swing by his office and pick up the cell phone, then by his apartment to take what few belongings he had with him. He thought he was still safe enough to make both stops. His cover had been blown, but even if Keller had seen Arlene's interview this morning on television and Nick's photo, he wouldn't be able to get here that fast.

Unless Keller had already gotten wind of where he was. That, Nick knew, had always been a possibility since Keller was out on bail with nothing to do but look for him.

His radio squawked.

"There's been another attempt on Arlene Evans's life," the dispatcher told him.

Nick swore silently. He couldn't deal with this now. He had to get out of town before it was too late. If it wasn't already. He could only guess how long his photo had been up on the Internet. Keller would have put the word out. Everyone would be on the lookout for Nicolas Giovanni.

"Arlene's under protective custody and doing fine," the dispatcher said. "You might want to come over to the jail though."

This surprised Nick. "Are you saying they caught the person who attacked Arlene?"

"One of the nurses caught her in the act. The deputy just took her down to the jail but he wanted me to let you know. It's Violet, Arlene's daughter."

Nick couldn't believe this. They already had the younger daughter locked up—and now her older sister?

"You aren't going to believe some of the stuff she's saying," the dispatcher said. "I think you'd better get over here."

AFTER LANEY HUNG UP from talking to her sister, she wiped her tears, angry with herself for crying, then threw herself into the physical labor of cleaning the kitchen until it shone.

Then she set about packing. She would drive to Billings and catch a flight home. She couldn't bear the thought of staying here another night alone. She'd seen the expression on Nick's face. He wouldn't be coming back.

She'd packed light to come to Montana. Unlike Laci who had four suitcases and had apparently brought most everything she owned. It didn't take long before Laney was ready to leave. She rolled her suitcase out to the porch and went back to make sure everything was turned off.

The sound of a vehicle set her heart racing. Her first thought, her most fervent wish, was that it would be Nick. He had tried to stay away but couldn't. He felt just as she did.

She ran through the house, slamming open the screen door and stopping short on the porch. She'd been ready to throw herself into Nick's arms. She didn't know why he was so afraid of this thing between them. She didn't care. As long as he didn't keep running.

But the car wasn't Nick's. Nor was the man who got out of the car Nick.

Laney looked into the face of a man she'd never seen before and knew instinctively his would probably be the last face she ever saw as he pulled a gun from beneath his jacket and pointed it at her heart.

"Let's step inside," the man said, coming up the porch stairs and grabbing her arm before she could move. He held the barrel of the gun to her temple. "You and I need to talk about our mutual friend, Nicolas Giovanni."

NICK FOUND TWO OF THE DEPUTIES in the interrogation room at the jail with Violet.

She was sitting at one end of the marred table looking as if she'd been invited to lunch rather than arrested for attempted murder.

He stepped into the room, and she looked up and smiled as if she'd been waiting for him. As far as he could tell she hadn't shed a tear. "Violet."

"Deputy Rogers," she said in response as he took a seat at the opposite end of the table and glanced at the deputies. They both seemed to shrug as if they couldn't quite believe this either.

"Want to tell me what's going on, Violet?" Nick asked, keeping his voice as calm as she appeared.

She met his gaze. There was a determination in hers, a resolve. "I tried to kill my mother this morning. I'm sorry that I failed again."

"So it wasn't the first time, I take it?" he asked, trying to keep his voice neutral.

"I tried before to smother her in the hospital, but I got interrupted. That time I managed to get away by hiding in a storage closet. I wasn't responsible for the other times we tried to kill her."

We? He stared at her for a moment, then pulled out his notebook and pencil even though he could see that the deputies had been videotaping her responses. He just needed a moment and this gave him the time.

"You say you were not responsible for the other times 'we' tried to kill her?" he finally asked.

"Those times it was Charlotte and Bo," she said matter-of-factly.

"Why don't you tell me about those times," he said.

And she did, starting with Maddie's and Bo's engagement party. It had been Charlotte's idea to poison their mother at the party with a macaroon. Violet's job had been to bake the cookie and make sure that only the poison cookie was left on the plate when Charlotte offered it to Arlene.

"So the macaroon was intended for your mother rather than Geraldine," he said.

"I felt sorry for Geraldine. Charlotte said we'd done her a favor." Violet shrugged.

"And Bo?"

"He didn't really care that Geraldine died except that now we would have to come up with another plan for Mother," she said.

"I meant, what part did Bo play in the other attempts on your mother's life?"

"Oh," she said. "He pushed Mother down the stairs. He pretended it was an accident. Mother forgave him of course. He was always her favorite."

"I would think that would be a good reason why he wouldn't want her dead," Nick pointed out. He noticed that the deputies seemed to be in shock as they listened and he suspected they'd already heard most of this.

"Bo hated her as much as we did. He hated her hanging on him, making so much of him, he was embarrassed by it. He just wanted her to go away." Violet's tone was such that she could have been talking about the weather or what to make for dinner instead of cold-blooded murder.

"And the overdose?"

"That was Charlotte. She put the pills in Mother's coffee."

"Where was your father when all this was going on?" Nick had to ask.

"He works all the time. I think he does it so he doesn't have to come in the house except to eat and sleep."

Nick took off his hat and raked a hand through his hair. He had to get moving, but he was so shocked by this that he couldn't help but ask the question that haunted him. "Why did you want your mother dead?"

"Me personally?" She met his gaze and smiled

ruefully. "Do you really have to ask? She would have married me off to Jack the Ripper if she could have. And since she couldn't marry me off to anyone, she made my life unbearable. I tried to find a husband just to get away from her but I couldn't. No one wanted me."

He heard the pain in her voice. "You know your sister has been arrested for assault," Nick said and explained why.

For the first time, Violet's eyes filled with tears. "I didn't know she was doing that." She bit her lip. "I didn't think anyone cared."

Nick didn't know what to say. He turned to one of the deputies. "Have you brought Bo Evans in yet?"

"We were waiting on word from you."

"Pick him up and you'd better call the county attorney and let him know what's going on." Nick shifted his gaze from the deputy to Violet. "I'm sorry you felt you had no recourse but to kill your mother."

She shrugged. "We did what we had to."

"Your mother is still alive," he said, not sure she knew that she and her siblings had failed yet another time.

Violet nodded. "At least for the moment."

Nick felt a chill in the room as he picked up his notebook and pen and rose from his chair. He wanted to be anywhere but in this room with this woman.

In his office, he sat down, felt the photographs Laney had given him in his shirt pocket. He took them out and tossed them on the desk, sick from what he'd heard in the interrogation room. Even sicker when he thought of Laney and the way he'd left things with her.

He glanced at his watch. He had to get moving. He should be hightailing it out of town. Keller would be on his trail. Even with Geraldine Shaw's murder solved and the after-hours bar assailant in jail, Nick felt he'd left too much undone.

One of the photographs caught his eye. He drew it closer. The snapshot was of Laney. She looked so beautiful. He wished he'd had the chance to dance with her that day.

Past Laney, he saw Charlotte caught in the act of taking something from her pocket and slipping it on the macaroon plate. Moments later Arlene would be offered the cookie, but Geraldine would take it before the murder weapon could reach the right victim. Life was so much chance. He shook his head and put down the photograph.

Soon all three of the Evans offspring would be in custody. He wondered how Arlene would take it. He suspected she would blame Violet. He used to hear cops debate whether it was the environment or the genes that eroded a family to the extent the kids were trying to kill one of their parents.

Hard to say. The bottom line was that as horrible as the Evanses were, they couldn't hold a candle to a guy like Zak Keller, who'd grown up on the same street as Nick, practically living with Nick's family.

Nick hurriedly unlocked the bottom drawer and took out his cell phone. Time to get the hell out of town. As he turned on the phone he saw that he had a message.

He played it and felt his blood run cold.

Chapter Thirteen

The man who called himself Zak Keller dragged
Laney into the kitchen and shoved her down into a
chair. He was tall and broad-shouldered with a sur-
prisingly handsome face and a full head of sandy-
blond hair cut in the latest style. He wore expensive
clothing, looked like a businessman, even smelled
good. On the surface, there appeared to be nothing
dangerous about him.

Until you looked into his eyes.

Zak Keller's were a colorless blue and totally
devoid of emotion. Soulless eyes.

"Here's the plan," he said in a voice as smooth as
any pricey attorney's. "You're going to call Nicolas.
You tell him I'm here to see him and that if he
doesn't do exactly what I want him to, I'll blow your
brains out. Can you remember that?"

It wasn't something she was likely to forget. Her
heart pounded so hard it made her chest hurt. She
was having trouble catching her breath and her mind

was like a caged squirrel, running too fast, going nowhere. She knew she had to calm down, had to think.

She stared at the man, absolutely positive he meant every word he'd said about blowing her brains out. "I can remember that," she said, surprised how calm she sounded.

He nodded and smiled at her. The smile of a shark just before it took a big bite.

Her logical mind argued that Zak Keller had the wrong man. She didn't know a Nicolas Giovanni. She knew a Nick Rogers, a deputy sheriff with a kind heart, a shy man, a man who was running from something.

She'd thought that something was her.

But now she had a bad feeling it was something much more dangerous. It was Zak Keller.

She fought not to show just how terrified she was. Especially of that little voice in her head that said Nick Rogers was Nicolas Giovanni. Nick had said he was Italian but that hadn't explained the last name Rogers. She'd seen the look on his face for that split second when he'd seemed to realize he'd given something away.

"You ready to make that call?" Zak Keller asked, glancing at his watch, then her.

"Yes," she said, aware that whatever Nick had been covering up was deadly serious. Otherwise she wouldn't have this man standing in her kitchen holding a gun on her, threatening to kill her.

"I left out one important point," Zak Keller said

as he handed her the phone. "If you try to warn anyone before you get Nicolas on the line, I will kill you. It doesn't make any difference to me really. I just thought this way would be more fun for Nicolas. We understand each other?"

She nodded and took the phone. As she dialed the sheriff's department number, he stepped closer and pressed the gun painfully into her temple, all the time smiling.

"Deputy Sheriff Nick Rogers please," she said when the dispatcher answered. Her voice sounded too high to her but Zak Keller didn't seem to notice.

"Just a moment."

Laney could hear the extension ringing. The way Nick had torn out of her house this morning, he could be miles away by now. She recalled how upset he'd been to see his face on national television. What had he done that would make him so afraid of having his picture on the Internet, on national television? Something that had a killer after him.

She could feel the man standing over her growing impatient. He'd planned to use her, but clearly he would just as easily change that plan by killing her first and going after Nick alone if he had to.

"Hello?"

Laney almost wept with relief at the sound of Nick's voice. "Nick."

ONE LITTLE WORD. But Nick heard everything he'd feared in that one word. He'd been on his way out of the office, hurrying after discovering the message on the cell phone in the locked bottom drawer. He wasn't sure what had made him turn back to answer the phone. Just a feeling…

"Laney, what—"

Zak Keller prodded her hard in the temple with the gun.

"I have a message for Nicolas Giovanni from Zak Keller," she said as evenly as she could. "He says if you don't do exactly what he wants, he is going to blow my brains out."

Her words struck Nick like a punch. The pain seared through him, burning him to his soul. For a moment, he couldn't speak, couldn't breathe. His heart had stopped, his mind stunned by the horror of even the thought of Zak Keller near Laney.

"You there, Nicolas?" Keller asked and laughed as he took the phone.

"I'm here," Nick said. He knew better than to demand that Keller let Laney go. Just as he knew better than to pretend she didn't matter to him. Unfortunately, he knew how Keller operated.

"Good. It's been too long. You've been a hard man to find."

Nick said nothing, waiting, his heart in his throat at what Keller would do to Laney.

"You and I need to get together, don't you think?"

"Only if Laney comes along," Nick said.

Keller laughed. "She isn't your usual type, my old friend. I thought you liked brunettes."

"I take what I can get."

Keller's laugh this time said he didn't buy Nick's nonchalance when it came to Laney, making Nick wonder how long he'd been in the area and just what he knew.

"How'd you find me?" Nick asked.

"Does it matter?"

"Just curious."

"Saw your picture on the Internet. It was the damnedest thing. It appeared you'd fallen in love," Keller said. "You really are a fast worker, old buddy. You got a cell phone?"

He knew Nick did. "You want the number?" Nick asked, but figured Keller already had it.

"Sure."

Nick rattled it off, wondering if Keller was even writing it down. If Keller already had the number then he'd taken out the one man Nick had trusted with his life. And now Nick had cost that man his life. Grief twisted inside him. How many more people had to die? But he knew the answer to that one. At least two.

"I'll call you and let you know where to meet us," Keller said. "But Nick, just in case you decide to do something stupid—"

The next thing Nick heard was Laney's scream. Hot flames of anger seared away the grief and desolation as the phone went dead. Nick threw the phone across the room. He saw the dispatcher looking toward his office. He had to pull himself together.

But his brain was screaming: *Keller has Laney. Keller has Laney.* Nothing on this earth could be as bad as that.

LANEY SCUTTLED ACROSS the floor trying to get away but Zak was on her, slamming her into the wall, slapping her again, making her cry out a second time.

Then smiling, he hung up on Nick.

"You can get up now," he said, his voice suddenly so calm it sent ice through her veins. "We're going for a little ride."

She struggled to her feet, her hand going to her mouth and coming away bloody. The bastard had split her lip—just to get a rise out of Nick.

Anger took the edge off her terror. Her brain seemed to start functioning again. She didn't want to go for a ride with him. If there was any way she could keep from getting into his car...

He had put the gun back into the holster as if he thought he no longer needed it and moved to replace the phone.

Her gaze took in the kitchen, seeing anything that she could use as a weapon. The knife rack was too far away. He'd be on her again before she could draw one, let alone use it on him, something she wasn't completely sure she could do anyway. A canister would be too awkward. Just as the large mixer or the toaster.

She staggered to the edge of the kitchen counter

and stopped. He half turned to glance back at her. She curled around herself, pretending to be more hurt than she was.

He turned his back to her again as he hung up the phone.

She grabbed the coffeepot from the coffeemaker. There was almost a full pot. She'd made it while she'd cleaned and got ready to leave and forgotten all about it. But the coffeemaker had kept it hot.

She moved swiftly, but he must have heard the pot scraping across the bottom of the coffeemaker. She was already running at him, the pot raised, when he spun around faster than she had anticipated.

She swung the pot with everything she had. His arm came up to block the blow. The pot shattered, sending hot coffee splattering across the kitchen— and the man.

He let out a bellow of pain and anger.

She never saw his other arm until it hit her, sending her sprawling backward across the room. She hit the wall; her head snapped back. Pain shot through her head just before everything went black.

NICK OPENED THE BOTTOM DRAWER of his desk, took out the cell and turned it on, then switched it with the phone on his belt that he'd been given when he'd taken the job.

He hated the way his hand shook. This was exactly what Keller wanted—him running scared.

But how could he not be terrified for Laney? Nick

knew what kind of man Zak Keller was. He'd seen how callous and cold-blooded the man could be. Nick knew what kind of danger Laney was in.

His mind raced with only one thought—saving Laney. From the beginning, Nick had known he probably wouldn't get out of this mess alive. At the very least, he would never be able to be a cop in California again. Keller had friends who would make sure of that.

But Laney hadn't asked for any of this. She deserved so much better. Nick would never forgive himself for jeopardizing her life. How had Keller found out about her? Because of last night?

Nick knew that couldn't be possible. Keller couldn't have known about them that quickly. Keller had said he'd found *him* and Laney on the Internet?

On impulse, Nick called up Arlene Evans's Meet-a-Mate Web site. He'd been so upset this morning at Laney's that he hadn't paid any attention to anything except the fact that Arlene and her damned site had made national television.

Now as he flipped through the photographs of the possible "dates," he saw what Keller must have seen—a photo of Nick and one of Laney with a stupid red heart around the two photographs and a caption that read True Love?

There were other photographs linked as well with stupid captions.

Nick felt sick. Arlene had no idea what she'd done. Not just to him. But to Laney. Arlene also had posted information about each of them. Keller wouldn't have had any trouble at all finding Laney.

Nick wanted to break something, to destroy the office, to curse God. But he knew that would just be a waste of time and property and spirit.

If he hoped to save Laney, he had to think like Keller. He had to be cold-blooded. He had to be calm. Mostly, if given the opportunity, he would have to be a killer.

In a separate locked drawer, he took out his own gun. He didn't have to check to see if it was loaded, but he did anyway. He needed to cover every base. He knew Keller would.

He grabbed two full clips and stuck them into the pocket of his denim jacket. From the drawer he took out his sheathed knife and slipped it into his boot.

Keller would expect him to be packing. He didn't want to let him down. His sheriff department-issue pistol that he'd been given when he took the job, he slipped into the holster, put on his denim jacket and, leaving the keys to the patrol car on his desk, left.

When he'd gotten to Whitehorse, he'd picked up an old used pickup. It was a beater, but it ran well. Since then, he'd been working so much he had barely used the truck.

But now he walked the four blocks to his apartment. It was one of a half-dozen built in a row, white with blue trim, neat as a pin.

Inside, he packed just for something to do while he waited for the call. He didn't have much. Everything fit into two duffel bags. He carried them out to the pickup and put them behind the seat.

Then he climbed behind the wheel, started the truck and drove down to Packy's to fill up with gas.

Keller hadn't called, but then he hadn't expected him to. Zak would try to drag this out as long as possible. He didn't just want to kill Nick; he wanted him to suffer.

Nick wouldn't let himself think about what might be happening to Laney. He couldn't or he would lose it. He had to keep his cool. Keller was hoping he would lose control, act on emotion rather than reason.

Not that Nick had a chance in hell. Keller would make sure of that. Nick was as good as dead. But maybe there was a chance for Laney. He concentrated on that.

On that and the thought that if he failed today, Keller would be free.

Nick couldn't let that happen. He'd had a chance once to kill Keller. He hadn't taken it. He wouldn't make that mistake again. But Keller might not give him another opportunity. In fact, Nick was pretty sure Keller wouldn't.

But maybe there was another way, he thought as he drove back to the sheriff's department. He checked out the video camera and new tape, went into his office and locked the door. It only took a few minutes to set up the camera; when the light came on, he sat down in front of the lens and began to speak.

"My name is Nicolas Giovanni. If you're watching this, I'm dead. As I make this recording, L.A. homicide detective Zak Keller has kidnapped Laney Cavanaugh. She might already be dead for all I know."

His voice threatened to break. He cleared his throat. "I was to testify against Zak Keller next week in a trial in Los Angeles. Since I don't think I'm going to be making that trial now, I'm giving my testimony by video. I saw Zak Keller kill two police officers in cold blood on May 31 of this year."

Nick took a breath and let it out and began again.

"I attempted to arrest him, but I was wounded and he got away. However, I did retrieve the gun he used and put it into evidence. The gun as well as the report verifying that his prints were on the weapon later disappeared, as did Zak. He was arrested but released on bail. After an attempt on my life, I went into hiding. Right now I am waiting for another call from Zak to tell me where to meet him." He shut off the camera and waited as the day turned to dusk, then dark.

When his cell phone rang, Nick turned the video camera back on and stepped closer. He let it ring another time, then answered it on camera.

"THAT YOU, OLD BUDDY?" Zak asked, amusement in his voice. "Took you long enough to answer. You playing games with me?"

Like you're playing games with me? "Couldn't get the damned thing out of my pocket," Nick said, wanting Zak to believe he was nervous. Hell, he was way beyond nervous.

Zak laughed. "Okay, here's the plan. You—"

"I need to know that Laney is still alive." He hoped the audio was picking up Zak's side of the conversation.

"You're in no position to make demands, Nicolas," Zak said, a sharp edge to his voice.

"Come on, Zak. Just let me hear her voice."

Silence. For a minute he thought Keller might have hung up.

"Just a minute. She's coming around."

Nick held his breath as he looked at the camera, saw the red recording light, waited to hear Laney's voice, terrified of what Keller had done to her.

"Nick, I'm all right."

She didn't sound all right.

"What has he done to you?"

"You want to hear the plan, Nick, or do you want to hear her scream? Your choice."

"Let's hear the plan, Zak."

"I'll have to call you back. Start driving north toward Saco."

"When does the killing stop, Zak?" Nick asked.

"You know the answer to that, old buddy. See you soon."

The line went dead. Nick looked at the camera, then walked over and shut it off, removed the cassette and put it in the padded envelope, addressed the video to the prosecuting attorney, Los Angeles, California. He gave the package to the dispatcher with instructions to overnight it the next morning.

Then he walked out to his pickup, climbed in and headed north toward Saco.

LANEY WOKE TO PANIC. She couldn't see a thing, but she realized at once that she was in a small dark place and she couldn't breathe. She tried to move but found her wrists and ankles bound, tape over her mouth.

She fought back the terror, sucking in air through her nose, as she realized where she was.

In the trunk of a car. She could hear the engine, the hum of the tires on the road, feel the rough carpet against her cheek as the car hit a bump, jostling her.

She lay curled in a fetal position. Her head ached and it took her a moment to remember what had happened. Zak Keller. She closed her eyes as fear overcame her.

Where was he taking her?

To meet Nick. Nicolas Giovanni.

Terror immobilized her worse than the tape that bound her. He was going to kill her. Except if that was all he had planned, he would have done it back at the house.

She felt the car slow, turn; the road became rough just before the car stopped in what felt like a few miles off the highway.

The engine died into silence. She held her breath as she heard the car door open, close, the sound of footsteps on gravel growing nearer.

The trunk lid popped open.

She blinked, blinded by the tiny trunk light overhead and surprised to see that it was dark outside. Even darker was the silhouette of Zak Keller standing over her.

"Laney Cavanaugh." His voice was as cold as his eyes. "Here, let me help you out."

The switchblade in his hand caught the light. She cringed as he brought it down. She heard his chuckle as he cut the tape that bound her ankles; then the blade disappeared, and he smiled and offered her his hand.

"I hope the ride wasn't too uncomfortable for you," he said.

He was just making conversation, clearly liking the sound of his own voice. He couldn't care less about her welfare and she knew it. She was a means to an end and she feared what that end was.

Her mouth was still covered with tape, her wrists still bound, as he helped her out of the trunk, then slammed the lid. They stood for a moment, him gripping her elbow.

She could make out structures, all dark. It wasn't until he led her toward the larger of the buildings that she recognized where they were. Sleeping Buffalo Resort. She'd heard that it was closed for repairs. Obviously so had Zak Keller.

At the door to the indoor pool, he shoved her into the corner. "Just stand there. We don't want another episode like back at the house, now do we?"

She said nothing, but she could see his expression. He wanted her to try to escape. He wanted to hurt her.

She watched him produce a crowbar and realized he'd had it in his other hand the entire time. Had she tried anything, she would have known about its existence much sooner.

As he worked quickly and with obvious expertise in breaking and entering, her mind raced. What were they doing here? She hated to imagine what he had planned for them. There was no doubt in her mind he would kill them. When he finished torturing them with whatever game he was playing.

Knowing that she had no chance of surviving gave her a kind of peace. Fear came with hope. She had no hope.

The wood around the door splintered. Zak Keller froze. She could tell he was listening. He knew no one was around or they wouldn't be here. He wasn't a man who left anything to chance. But he also knew there could always be surprises, unplanned contingencies.

No one came at the sound of the wood splintering. Nor when he pushed the door open and dragged Laney inside. She smelled the heavy damp scent of the mineral pool. Their footsteps echoed on the concrete floor as he led her past the desk into the huge pool area.

The ceiling was high, the echo of their footfalls on the concrete louder in here. She could hear the gurgle of the water at the inlets as they skirted the pool. It was pitch-black inside the massive room, but she could make out a faint light coming from the locker rooms.

He drew her toward the light in the women's locker room, down the narrow entry past the old-fashioned wire baskets with numbers on them, around the corner to the line of dressing rooms.

He stopped in front of one and drew back the plastic shower curtain to expose a bench. "Sit."

She sat. The switchblade appeared again. He sliced the blade through the duct tape around her wrists. She rubbed at her sore red skin, trying not to imagine what was coming next.

"Okay, here's the deal," he said leaning over her. "You're going to call your boyfriend and tell him to come get you. But if you scream, which would be stupid on your part since there isn't anyone around for miles, but if you do, I will hurt you. We understand each other?"

Perfectly, she thought, and nodded.

He jerked the tape off her mouth. She couldn't help the small cry of pain. He smiled, taking pleasure in her pain, no matter how small. Then he took out the cell phone, dialed a number and handed her the phone.

It rang three times. She could see Zak Keller growing impatient again. If Nick was smart he would be miles away from here by now. He wouldn't come out here. Why get them both killed?

"Hello."

The sound of his voice brought both relief and regret. "Nick." She cleared her throat, her gaze on Zak. He looked ready to hurt her as if balancing on the edge of a knife blade, ready to go off at any minute. "He wants you to come out to Sleeping Buffalo."

"Do whatever he tells you to," Nick said, his voice sounding almost too calm. "Don't give him an excuse to hurt you."

"Ask him if he knows where the pool is," Zak ordered.

"Do you know where the swimming pool is?" she asked.

"I'm on my way."

Something in his voice tore at her heart. "Don't. Run. He's going to—"

Zak slammed her against the side of the dressing-room wall.

She was ready for the blow and made no sound.

The phone clattered to the floor. Calmly Zak picked it up, glaring at her, disappointed that she hadn't screamed for Nick's benefit.

"How do you inspire such loyalty?" Zak asked Nick as he spoke into the phone. "She risks my wrath to save your sorry ass. You're really something, Nicolas. But then you always did have a way with the ladies, didn't you? We'll be waiting for you." He disconnected and looked at Laney.

She could tell he wanted to hit her again. She met his gaze, held it; seconds passed.

"Take off your clothes."

Chapter Fourteen

"I said, take off your clothes," Zak Keller ordered. "I can rip them off if you like, but then you might get more than you bargained for if that happens."

Laney looked into his eyes. She hadn't bargained for any of this and he knew it. In the depths of those soulless eyes, she saw evil as dark and sinister as the pits of hell.

"Oh come on," he snapped. "I'm not going to rape you." He shook his head and chuckled. "Don't get me wrong. I'm tempted. But there isn't time. Nick won't know that I didn't though. It will drive him crazy to think that I had you." He pulled out the gun and pointed it at her head. "Or Nick can find you slumped in a pool of your own blood in this dressing room. Your choice."

"Why are you doing this?" she asked as she slowly began to take off her shoes and socks.

"Nick didn't tell you? No, I guess he wouldn't. Nick and I were partners." He motioned with the gun for her to speed up the disrobing.

"Partners?" she asked as she put her shoes and socks aside and began to unbutton her blouse, trying to imagine what kind of business dealings Nick would have had with this man.

"Homicide detectives," Zak Keller said.

"*You* were a *cop?*" She couldn't hide her shock.

His laugh had a sharp edge to it. "I'm *still* a cop. Nick is trying to take that away from me, but it will be over my dead body." Anger made the veins in his forehead pop out. The hand holding the gun was trembling and she could see that he was having trouble controlling his anger.

She let her blouse drop to the floor. "You were partners?" she said in an attempt to calm him down.

"Partners," he repeated and took a moment before he said, "We were from the same neighborhood. We grew up together as close as any real brothers before we became brothers in blue. Only Nicolas forgot about the code."

"The code?" She began to unbutton her jeans.

"The code that no matter what happens on the job, cops stick together. Nick broke the code."

"So you were police officers in Houston together?"

"Houston? Is that what he told you?" Zak laughed. "L.A. He hasn't been very truthful with you."

No, Nick hadn't. But if Zak was any indication, she was beginning to understand why.

She slipped out of her jeans, leaving her bra and panties on. She could feel those cold pale eyes on her.

"So he never mentioned me?" Zak asked. "I'm deeply hurt. I'll have to tell him when I see him. I used to spend more time with his family than with my own. He tell you about his family? No? A big Italian family."

So at least that much was true.

"Come on, take the rest of it off. You don't have anything I haven't seen before." He glanced toward the pool. "I'm worried about Nicolas. Calling himself Rogers. The way he loves old Roy Rogers westerns, didn't he realize that name would set off alarms with me? New deputy sheriff in town. Linked romantically with pretty local girl. That is all so Nick." Zak laughed. "He always was a sucker for those sappy happy endings."

Laney slipped out of her panties, then her bra. She shivered, crossed her arms over her bare chest, and raised her eyes slowly to meet Zak Keller's. She knew he'd be grinning. He was.

"Now that wasn't so bad, was it?"

She said nothing, holding his gaze.

"Put your arms down," he ordered.

She did, refusing to look away as she felt his gaze slide over her body like slime. It took all her composure not to strike out at him. But she knew he would have enjoyed that too much.

There was no getting past him, not with him blocking the narrow opening of the dressing room. He had her trapped. Trying to fight him would only play right into his hands.

His grin broadened as his gaze returned to hers. "I think I'm beginning to understand now what Nicolas saw in you." He reached into his pocket with his free hand and pulled out the duct tape. "Sorry, but I'm going to have to tape your wrists again."

She glared at him, making him chuckle, as she stuck out her hands.

He grabbed them, putting the gun back into his pocket as he taped her wrists together tightly.

She didn't make a sound, holding in the pain, determined not to give him the satisfaction.

When he'd finished, he ripped off a piece of tape and, staring into her eyes as he did it, slapped it across her mouth. "Nicolas will be here soon. We're almost ready." His gaze dropped to her left breast before coming back up to hers. With his eyes locked on hers, he reached over and pinched her nipple hard.

She cried out before she could stop herself. It came out a muffled sound behind the tape.

Zak Keller smiled. "*Now* we're ready."

NICK TURNED OFF THE HIGHWAY just south of Saco. He'd been out this way before. Next to the road was a small enclosed area like a manger. Inside was a large brown rock that some thought resembled a sleeping buffalo. The rock was sacred to the Native Americans in the area. That was why it was covered with tobacco, their offerings.

There was a story that the rock had once been

moved into Whitehorse, but each morning the massive rock would be facing the opposite direction it had the night before. Spooked by this, the rock had been returned to where it had been found and later put in this shelter.

Nick drove down the road toward Nelson Reservoir and Sleeping Buffalo Resort, fear making his mouth dry and his heart ache. If Zak hadn't taken Laney, Nick would have gone in, guns blazing. But Laney changed everything. That was why Zak had abducted her. But why bring her here?

The pool was closed, the large interior dark. Nick parked next to what he assumed was Keller's rental car. As he neared the building, he saw that the door had been pried open. He pushed on it, staying to one side.

He didn't really expect an ambush. Keller didn't work that way. He preferred theatrics. Zak had always kidded him about his love of old westerns. And yet Zak had planned an old-fashioned shoot-out here in this 1930s resort.

Nick listened. He could hear the soft lap of water, a sound like a fist to his belly. Keller hadn't just randomly chosen this place. He knew about Nick's fear of water. Early in his career, he'd been in pursuit of a felon and fallen through a rotten pier to be trapped underwater until rescued by some bystanders. The incident had left him afraid of water.

LANEY STOOD SHIVERING in the dark beside the pool. Zak had hold of her arm, his fingers digging into her flesh. She'd heard the car drive up, heard the engine shut off, the car door open. Then there had been nothing but silence.

She could feel the tension in the cop's grip. He'd taken the gun out of his pocket again before he'd led her out to the pool. She noted the way he stood just a little behind her as if he planned to use her as a shield should Nick come in firing.

Laney thought of her sister and her grandparents. It tore out her heart to think that she would never see them again. She feared that the news of her death would kill her grandmother Pearl and devastate her grandfather Titus. She couldn't bear to imagine what it would do to Laci. They had always been so close.

Fear threatened to paralyze her. Once they'd reached the side of the pool, Zak had taped her ankles together. She'd always been a strong swimmer but with her wrists and ankles taped together, she feared she wouldn't be able to keep her head above water. There was no doubt in her mind that she would end up in the pool. Why else would Zak Keller choose this place?

NICK CREPT ALONG THE EDGE of a short stone wall that opened into the pool area. He could hear the slap of the water against the sides of the pool, smell the hot water and feel the steam coming off the surface brush past his face.

He took deep breaths, caught between his fear and his anger. He could see the clear path of how his life had led him to this very spot, to this dark night, to this deserted pool. He'd seen things in Zak that had worried him even when they were kids. The barely concealed rage. The troubled kid from down the block with the alcoholic father, the whore mother. He'd seen the bruises on Zak, bruises his friend had always passed off as clumsiness.

Nick had known better, but he'd let Zak save face. Nick's family had practically adopted Zak, giving him a safe place to come when things were bad at his house, feeding him, even clothing him with hand-me-downs from all the cousins.

Zak had said he wanted to be a cop from the time they were just kids. Nick had fought his family legacy, but Zak had been so persuasive, telling Nick that Zak needed his head at the academy. Nick had helped Zak with his grades; Zak had helped him on the firing range.

Nick remembered the day they'd gotten hired. The picture of the two of them in their uniforms sat on the mantel at Nick's parents' home. Nick and Zak smiling at the camera. Zak so proud. It was the same year that Zak's father had taken his life and Zak's mother had run off, never to be seen again.

Nick shoved away the memories as he crouched behind a section of the stone wall. All the signs had been there. The violent arrests, the warnings, the growing distance between him and his partner.

And then the night that Nick had watched Zak kill two police officers from another precinct over a drug bust that had gone haywire. Zak had blamed the two cops for ruining his perfect bust record.

For months Nick had feared it would come to this. Laws and trials weren't for men like Zak Keller. He believed he was above the law. This was Zak Keller's idea of justice, killing anyone who crossed him. Even his once best friend.

"Zak?" Nick called, staying low behind the wall.

No answer. Water dripped nearby and lapped at the edge of the pool.

"Keller, you wanted me here, now show yourself."

A low chuckle came from the other side of the pool. "I wasn't sure you'd come," Keller said. A lie. Zak wouldn't have taken Laney unless he knew he could use her as leverage.

"Where's Laney?" Nick called.

"She's around. First get rid of your gun."

Nick pulled out his service revolver and tossed it down the concrete apron around the pool. The gun clattered across the floor, coming to a stop at the far end of the building.

"Any more weapons you'd like to be rid of?" Keller asked, then chuckled. "I didn't think so. There's a light switch off to your left. Why don't you turn it on?"

Nick could think of two good reasons why that would be a bad idea. Fear of what he would see was at the top of the list. Followed quickly by a bullet. Not a killing one. Just a maiming one.

"I want to know that Laney's all right first," he called back.

"You never had any faith, you know that? It was one of your flaws."

"Faith? I had all the faith in the world in you, Zak. I trusted you with my life." He felt anger rear its ugly head. It felt good. Better than fear. Keller wanted him to be afraid. "You betrayed me before you even betrayed yourself and every other cop."

"Nicolas, Nicolas, if I wanted a sermon I would have gone to church."

Nick heard the shuffle of feet on the other side of the pool where the locker rooms were.

"Your girlfriend is here now. Say something to him," Keller ordered.

There was the sound of tape being ripped off, then "Nick?" Laney's voice sounded tight. "What's going on?"

"Didn't you tell her, Nick? Ah, I'm disappointed in you. All that talk about honesty and you let her walk into something like this cold?"

"It's okay, Laney. I'll give him what he wants and he'll let you go."

"I really doubt that, Nick. He—"

Nick heard a struggle. It was all he could do-not to make a run through the dark in the hopes of getting to the other side before Keller could get to a light and take a clear shot at his target.

But before Nick could move, he heard a splash.

"Okay, here's the deal, Nicolas. Your girlfriend just went for a swim in the deep end of the pool. Her hands and feet are taped together. Now turn on the light, Nick, before she drowns."

Chapter Fifteen

Laney went under. The dark water rushed around her. She'd had only an instant to grab a breath before Zak had shoved her in. She was naked, her wrists and ankles bound, the tape back on her mouth. She sank to the bottom and struggled to kick back to the surface.

The pool at this end was no more than ten feet deep. But even if it had been six, she knew she still could drown in it. She fought her way to the surface, kicking her feet in tandem like a mermaid's tail. It was awkward and tiring.

She surfaced, took a huge gulp of air through her nose and went under again. For that moment though, she'd seen Zak standing at the edge of the pool, the gun in his hand. He hadn't paid any attention to her. His gaze had been on the far wall of the pool where the entrance was. He'd been trying to see Nick in the darkness.

Laney knew she had to get to the side of the pool—the farthest away from Zak Keller. She pushed off the bottom, aiming herself toward the closest side away from him—the side with the diving board, the deepest part of the pool.

She kicked with all her might, surfaced and sucked in air. She still had a half-dozen feet to go. Her head went under. She sank back down to the bottom again, knowing it was her only hope. The swimming was tiring her out. She wasn't sure how much longer she could manage to surface.

NICK'S HEART WAS IN HIS THROAT. Seconds were ticking by. He could hear Laney struggling in the water. He would kill Keller if it was the last thing he did. He should have killed him that night when he'd realized that Keller wasn't just a bad cop; he was the worst kind of cop.

But Nick had believed in the law. He'd tried to arrest his partner instead. A huge mistake with Nick still shocked by what he'd witnessed and Keller taking full advantage of it.

Keller was convinced he could do anything he wanted and get away with it. And so far he had.

Nick swore under his breath as he felt vital seconds tick past. He had no choice. He had to save Laney. But turning on the light would only get them both killed and he knew it. He knew Keller. He knew what he was capable of. The blinders were off. It was kill or be killed.

"Okay," he called to Keller. "Let me find the light."

Nick hurriedly pulled off his boots and jacket, slipped his own gun into the shoulder holster and, taking the knife from the sheath, crept along the stone wall until he was near the diving board at the deep end. He'd gone in the opposite direction that Keller had told him to.

He could hear Laney thrashing in the water a few yards away. He just prayed she was managing to get to the surface enough to get a breath of air.

"I can't find the light," Nick said.

"You went the wrong way. You never could tell your left from your right," Keller said and chuckled at what a fool Nick was.

Nick had always played that part between the two of them. *Naive,* Keller used to call him. "As much crap as you've seen, you still want to believe that human nature is inherently good," Zak would say then laugh. "You're a prize, Nicolas. A real prize."

With the knife in his hand, Nick dove into the pool at the deep end.

The heavily rich mineral hot springs water was a dark tea color. He knew he had only a matter of seconds to get to Laney, cut her free and fire.

He opened his eyes under the water and saw nothing in the darkness of the pool. But he knew any moment Keller would go for the lights and, once he did, Nick would be his target.

Light suddenly shimmered overhead on the surface of the pool. Nick could see Laney just inches from him. She was fighting to surface. He came up next to her, dragging her toward the edge of the pool under the diving board as he cut the tape binding her hands and pressed the knife into her palm before reaching to draw his gun from his holster.

The gun was gone.

Nick looked up to find Keller kneeling over him at the edge of the pool, the dark barrel end of a .357 Magnum pointing at his head.

"You son of a bitch," Zak said grinning. "That was one nice stunt. You always were one crazy mother—" He swung the barrel, caught Nick in the temple; the light overhead dimmed and threatened to go out as his head was shoved underwater.

LANEY RIPPED THE TAPE from her mouth with her free hand and coughed as she gasped for air and clung to the side of the pool with the hand holding the knife.

Her lungs ached. She'd swallowed too much water. Her limbs felt weak from the hot water, the terror and waning adrenaline.

She saw Zak Keller hit Nick, saw him push Nick under. She was just yards away from where Zak stood at the edge of the pool. She gripped the knife in her hand, forgetting for a moment that her ankles were still bound together.

Nick surfaced, coughing, his hand going to his head. She could see blood streaming down his face from the cut just over his left eye. He looked dazed as he made a swipe at the blood.

Hurriedly, Laney struggled to get the blade of the knife between her bare ankles to cut the thick tape.

As weak as she was, it took both hands. As she finally got the blade between her ankles and began to saw, she slid down the side of the pool to the bottom.

The knife felt awkward in her hands. She was trembling, straining to cut the tape, needing air as if her lungs would never get enough oxygen ever again.

She felt Nick's hand as he reached for her and looked up to see him floating underwater just above her. The water around him was dark with his blood.

She couldn't stay down any longer. Her lungs were on fire. She had to surface. She had to surface *now*.

The knife blade slipped. She felt the blade nick her skin but she ignored the pain as she jerked the blade hard upward, cutting the heavy thick tape with the last of her strength. The sticky tape still bound her legs. She had to drop the knife to get the tape off.

As she bent, her vision starting to dim from lack of oxygen, she saw the gun. It lay on the bottom of the pool. Almost within reach.

ZAK KELLER GRABBED Nick's shirt and jerked him to the surface. "Nicolas, Nicolas, what were you thinking? Oh, I know, you just had to play hero. Save the girl. Save your soul."

"You think killing me is going to make all that trouble back home go away?" Nick asked as he tried to catch his breath. Blood ran into his left eye. He blinked up at Zak.

He'd seen Laney underwater struggling to cut the tape. He wanted to reach for her, but knew that would only call attention to her. It would be just like Keller to shoot her now, now that Nick could watch. After all, if he knew Keller, and he did, that was exactly what the cop planned to do.

"They'll be watching you," Nick said, moving in the water to block Zak's view of Laney. "You'll always be under suspicion."

"Thanks to you," Keller snapped and pointed the barrel of the gun between Nick's eyes. "Why didn't you leave well enough alone? What were those cops to you? Nothing." He shook his head. "Dammit, Nick, you and I were partners, hell, we were bros." He sounded close to tears. "I loved you, man. You were family."

"Yeah, but we didn't know then that you got all the criminal genes in the family."

"Funny, Nicolas. You always were a barrel of laughs." He glared down at him. "I'm trying to tell you I didn't want it to end like this. How can you still buy into all that bureaucracy bull? Justice goes to the highest bidder. You think I was the only cop on the take?" He laughed. "You have no idea."

"It wasn't just that you were on the take," Nick said. "You killed two *cops*." Next to him, a strip of duct tape floated up. Laney had managed to free her ankles. So why hadn't she surfaced?

Zak was watching *him*, not her. What was she doing down there? He could feel the water move.

She was swimming but apparently not toward the surface. What the hell?

And that was when it hit him. She must have seen his gun on the bottom. Was going down for it. He wanted to scream "Don't do it!" Laney didn't know Keller. He'd shoot her before she could figure out how to fire the gun.

He swam a little closer to Zak even though he knew it was dangerous. But Nick had to be ready the moment Laney surfaced. He'd have to go for Zak before Zak could kill her.

"Go ahead, kill me," Nick said. "That is why you came all this way, wasn't it? So what's stopping you? Oh, did I mention that I made a videotape and recounted everything? About seeing you kill those cops, about you taking Laney Cavanaugh, about you planning to kill us both. I even taped your phone call to me telling me where to meet you."

Keller's bravado slipped a little, then his eyes narrowed, but all his attention was on Nick. "And you dropped it in overnight mail? Nicolas, nice touch, but I have friends in the county attorney's office. That little package will never reach anyone who can hurt me."

He cocked the gun. "And you're right. There isn't any reason to put this off any longer. I'd hoped that I could talk you into changing your story, but I can see that I'd be wasting my breath." He aimed the gun at Nick's forehead, his finger on the trigger. "Goodbye, Nicolas."

THE GUN WAS HEAVIER THAN LANEY had expected it to be. She brought it up close to her face. The lack of oxygen was making her light-headed. She had to surface, but when she did she knew she had to be ready to pull the trigger.

She knew a little about guns. Her grandfather Titus had taught both her and Laci to shoot when they were younger. He said it was important to have a healthy respect for guns.

This model had a clip. She couldn't be sure there was a cartridge in the chamber. She pulled back the slide and let it go. All she had to do was pull the trigger when she surfaced. She slipped her finger through the trigger guard and looked up. Air. Her body felt like lead.

She shoved off the bottom with both feet, her hands holding the gun trembling as she shot toward the surface, her eyes open. She knew she would get only one chance. If she missed, she was dead. And so was Nick. They were probably both dead anyway.

She brought the gun up, fighting to keep her hands steady as she burst to the surface, gulped air and pulled the trigger. The boom resounded, echoing like thunder across the pool. She fired again just before she went under. Or at least she heard a shot. Then another and another.

It wasn't until then that she felt the pain and knew she'd been hit.

Nick grabbed for Zak the moment he felt the water change behind him, the moment he heard Laney surface and fire. All he could reach as he lunged out of the water was Zak's leg. He grabbed hold and jerked as hard as he could.

A gunshot boomed in the big barnlike room, echoing across the water.

Zak lost his footing, falling backward, coming down hard on the edge of the pool. Another shot rang out as Nick jerked Zak into the water and grabbed for his gun.

Zak had recovered from hitting the edge of the pool. Either that or he was running on high-octane anger. Nick didn't remember him ever being so strong as they struggled for the gun, both going under the water. Nick could see that he'd been wounded by the shots Laney had fired. But still Zak fought like a man obsessed.

Nick was running out of air. His head ached from where he'd been hit and he knew he'd lost a lot of blood. He needed to surface. He managed to wrestle the gun from Zak but as he swam toward the surface, his lungs bursting, Zak made a grab for the gun.

Zak had cocked the gun before hitting the water. His finger hooked through the trigger guard as he fought to turn the barrel end away from himself and at Nick. The gun went off. Nick felt the report and looked down an instant before he surfaced. He saw the expression on Zak's face, saw the surprise, the pain, the realization.

BLOOD FLOATED ON TOP of the water like an oil slick. Laney hung on the side of the pool, fighting for air, fighting against the pain in her side. She cupped her hand over the wound.

She had seen movement just under the water. The surface of the water was rough, the waves lapping at the side of the pool, the air thick with steam.

Her vision began to blur. She felt her hand holding on to the side of the pool slip. Her head went under. She grasped for the edge of the pool, the pain in her side excruciating. She knew she had to get out of the water, get help.

Her eyes were open. She could see something on the bottom of the pool. A body. Nick?

Laney felt hands lifting her. She was rising through the water toward the light. She could see the rough surface of the pool above her, the light growing brighter and brighter until her head burst through. She took a huge gulp of air, then another. And then she saw that the man holding her was Nick.

Relief mixed with the pain and the fear and came out in rattling sobs.

"It's okay, baby," he breathed against her neck as he drew her through the water toward the shallow end of the pool. "It's okay. I'm here now. I'm here."

She clung to him as the light overhead dimmed, then blacked out.

Chapter Sixteen

Nick stayed by Laney's side in the ambulance and helicopter that airlifted her to Billings. Doctors had insisted on stitching the cut over his left eye while he waited for her to come out of surgery for a gunshot wound to her side.

He was exhausted, but he couldn't sleep. He kept remembering the limp feel of Laney in his arms and Zak's body lying in the dark water at the bottom of the pool.

Nick hadn't been to church since he was a boy, but he prayed that Laney would survive. He couldn't bear the thought of losing her, even though he knew that once she regained consciousness she wouldn't want anything to do with him. He couldn't blame her. This was all his fault. He would never forgive himself.

Just before daylight, Laney opened her eyes. He moved to her side, taking her hand, relief closing off his throat, making his eyes tear. All he could do was smile down at her. She squeezed his hand, then closed her eyes again.

The doctor came into the room and told him Sheriff Carter Jackson was waiting for him in the hall.

Nick kissed Laney on the forehead and went out to face Sheriff Jackson, who he'd heard had returned from Florida to find his jail full and a dead man at the bottom of a swimming pool.

"I've got a lot of questions," Jackson said. He had two deputies with him. "And when you're through answering them for me, it seems you're wanted in California to answer a whole bunch more."

Nick nodded and glanced back toward Laney's room. He didn't want to leave her, but he could tell if he refused, Jackson was ready to arrest him.

"The doctor said it looks like she's going to pull through just fine," Jackson said, following Nick's gaze down the hall to Laney Cavanaugh's room. He eyed the stitched-up cut over Nick's left eye. "Meanwhile, you're going to have to come with me."

Nick didn't need Sheriff Jackson to tell him he was in a world of trouble. It was his word against Zak's about what had happened the night the two cops had been killed. Zak had used what cops called a "throw-down" gun to kill them. It had been untraceable to Zak and now that gun with Zak's fingerprints was missing.

The only hope Nick had was the videotape he'd

made. If Zak's voice was on there, it might prove that Nick had killed Zak in self-defense.

He didn't want Laney to have to testify. Sheriff Jackson would take her statement and send it on to California.

Nick hoped that would be the end of her involvement. Zak Keller still had friends in California. Nick was determined never to risk Laney's life again.

LANEY AGREED TO RETURN to Old Town Whitehorse to recuperate and let her sister and grandfather look after her. What had happened still felt like a bad nightmare. When she'd awakened in the hospital, drugged and in pain, she'd been disappointed not to see Nick.

She must have dreamed it, but she thought she remembered him beside her bed the first time she'd woken up. She remembered the feel of a kiss on her forehead.

Her doctor had told her Nick had left with a sheriff from Whitehorse. She'd heard since that Nick had returned to L.A. where he was being questioned on the death of Zak Keller and two policemen killed eight months before. He was on suspension from the police force in L.A. until after the case went to trial.

The grapevine hummed with all the news. Rumors abounded. She heard that Nick was really a spy for the CIA. She also heard that he was with the FBI and had been working undercover in Whitehorse.

The publicity had been great for Sleeping Buffalo Resort, which had opened again to record crowds.

"How are you feeling?" Laci asked as she joined Laney on the porch.

"Fine." Laney looked out at the open country. It was late September. They'd had a cool spell but today was hot, the sky cloudless and a blinding blue.

"I'm baking you some sugar cookies," Laci announced. "You know the kind you like with white icing and sprinkles?"

"You keep cooking for me like this and I'll be as round as a beach ball," Laney said. The truth was she felt guilty because she barely ate. She'd lost her appetite and wondered if she would ever be hungry again.

"You sure you feel all right?" Laci asked, sounding worried.

Laney reached over to squeeze her sister's hand. "You know the doctor said the wound has healed just fine. He said if I stay here much longer it will be considered malingering."

"It's Nick, isn't it?" Laci said.

Laney turned away to look down the road, hating the tears that welled in her eyes. She had such mixed feelings about Nick. She'd gotten most of the real story from Sheriff Jackson. She understood why Nick had lied about his name, where he was from, who he really was.

Except she'd fallen in love with Nick Rogers, the man she'd thought he was. She didn't know Nick Giovanni from L.A.

"He called again," Laci said as the timer went off

on the oven in the kitchen and her sister rose to get her cookies out before they burned.

Laney nodded. She hadn't felt up to talking to him. In truth, she didn't know what to say. She was sure by now that he'd returned to his job as a homicide detective. She'd heard he'd been reinstated now that everything had been cleared up. She'd offered to go to L.A. and testify if the county attorney needed more than her statement. But the video Nick had made the night she'd been abducted by Zak Keller had been crucial in ending the case.

"I think you should talk to Nick," Laci said.

"I think you'd better see to my cookies." Laney smiled when she said it.

"He's in love with you," Laci said as the timer went off again. "Any fool could see that," she called as she scrambled back into the house to save the cookies she'd baked.

Laney found herself looking down the road. She knew she would never be the same. The doctor had said it was normal considering the trauma she'd been through.

She smiled at that now. As terrified as she'd been every moment with Zak Keller, that paled next to the real ordeal she'd experienced this summer. She'd fallen in love and now her heart was breaking at even the thought that she would never see Nick Rogers again.

She knew that was why she didn't take Nick's calls. He was back in L.A., back with his family, back being Nicolas Giovanni. The trauma she'd experienced was the death of Nick Rogers, the man she'd fallen in love with one summer day in the middle of Montana.

She'd been staring down the road so long that at first she thought she'd just imagined the small cloud of dust on the horizon. She watched the dust billow up, the cloud growing larger as the vehicle approached. She told herself it was probably bad news.

Whitehorse had been rocked when the story had come out about the Evans offspring. Arlene was still in denial. At least when it came to Bo and Charlotte. She had gotten both of them lawyers. Now Bo and Charlotte were swearing it had all been Violet's idea, including the attack on the men outside the bar. Laney suspected Arlene had persuaded them to say that so she didn't lose all her children.

Violet had had to be taken to a maximum-security jail in Great Falls after she'd attacked both of her siblings in court. Word around town was that Violet would be taken to the mental hospital in Warm Springs for evaluation. No one expected her ever to stand trial. Arlene had already gotten both Bo and Charlotte out on bail.

Laney stared down the road as the sun glinted off the roof of a car she didn't recognize. Her heart kicked up a beat, her pulse a drum in her ears, as the car pulled to a stop in front of the house.

She couldn't see the driver, not with the sun ricocheting off the windshield, half blinding her.

She watched as the driver's side door slowly opened and like a mirage, Nick stepped out.

He hesitated as he looked across the hood of the car at her. He wore a gray Stetson, jeans, a western shirt and boots. She found she couldn't speak as he closed the car door and started up the steps. Laney caught a whiff of warm sugar cookies and Nick's all-male scent, the two mixing into a smell that would be forever branded in her memory.

Nick stepped into the cool shade of the porch, pulled off his hat, turned the brim nervously in his fingers as his gaze met hers. "I'm sorry but I had to see you."

She found her voice. "I'm glad you came." Tears burned her eyes as she pushed herself out of her chair, drawn to him like metal to a magnet.

He stepped toward her saying, "Please, don't get up." But she was already on her feet, already headed for his arms. He opened them and pulled her in, burying his face in her hair.

NICK FELT THE SMALL QUIET shudders of her sobs as he held her, afraid to hold her too tightly for fear of hurting her. He'd talked to her doctors, been assured that the bullet from Zak's gun had gone all the way through her side and hadn't hit any vital organs. That she had healed just fine.

But Nick knew from experience what it was like to come back from a gunshot wound. The trauma wasn't all in the flesh. And after what Laney had been through, even as strong as he knew her to be, he worried that she might never heal.

"I'm so sorry," Nick said against her hair.

She shook her head and drew back, wiping her eyes before looking up at him. "The sheriff told me everything. It wasn't your fault."

"I should never have looked twice at you," he said, then felt himself soften. "But I couldn't help myself."

She smiled through her tears. "I know the feeling."

He heard the screen door squeak open a crack behind him. "I have Laney's favorite sugar cookies and iced tea if either of you are interested," Laci said from the doorway.

Nick grinned as he met Laney's gaze. "Maybe in a little while. I need to talk to your sister first."

"Okay, well, maybe I'll make some homemade ice cream," Laci said and shut the door.

"There's a lot I want to tell you," Nick said, thinking about his best friend Danny O'Shay, about growing up in the streets of L.A., about Zak and everything that had happened culminating in the swimming pool the night she'd been shot.

But all that could wait. "The Whitehorse sheriff has offered me my old job. He kept it open in case I wanted to come back," Nick told her. "Amazingly, he thinks I make a pretty good deputy sheriff. He doesn't realize I had a lot of help solving the local crimes while he was in Florida."

Laney was staring up at him. "I thought your life was in California?"

"I have a huge Italian family in L.A., but none of them have ever been to Montana so I suspect there will be a constant flow of parents and uncles and aunts and cousins for years to come if I stay here," he said.

"Are you telling me you're actually thinking of taking your old job back?" She still sounded disbelieving.

"I told Carter I had to think about it. That it was contingent on you."

"Me?" Laney asked, her voice breaking.

"You said once that you wouldn't mind staying here if you met the right man. I'm not saying I'm the right man. But I sure as the devil would like to try to be that man. If it isn't too late. If you think you could ever trust me after everything that's happened. If you—"

Laney touched her finger to his lips and laughed. It felt good to laugh. Just as it had felt wonderful to be in Nick's arms again.

"Why don't you just kiss me and let's see what happens," she said.

"This from the woman with the analytical mind?" he said as he reached for her.

His kiss was everything Laney remembered and more. She opened to him, surrendering to a man named Nick Giovanni, a man she felt as if she'd just met. The woman who always looked before she leaped, just jumped right in.

She told herself they had time to get to know each other, as she heard Laci in the kitchen making ice cream. Later they would sit on the porch and watch the sun go down as they ate sugar cookies and homemade ice cream together.

She remembered her restlessness at the beginning of her summer visit. As Nick deepened the kiss, she knew she would never be restless again. Not as long as Nick was around. It was good to be home. As that old saying went, home is definitely where the heart is. And her heart was right at home here in Montana.

* * * * *

Every Life Has More
Than One Chapter™

Award-winning author Stevi Mittman delivers another hysterical mystery, featuring Teddi Bayer, an irrepressible heroine, and her to-die-for hero, Detective Drew Scoones. After all, life on Long Island can be murder!

*Turn the page for a sneak peek
at the warm and funny fourth book,
WHOSE NUMBER IS UP, ANYWAY?,
in the Teddi Bayer series,
by STEVI MITTMAN.
On sale August 7*

"Before redecorating a room, I always advise my clients to empty it of everything but one chair. Then I suggest they move that chair from place to place, sitting in it, until the placement feels right. Trust your instincts when deciding on furniture placement. Your room should "feel right."
—TipsFromTeddi.com

Gut feelings. You know, that gnawing in the pit of your stomach that warns you that you are about to do the absolute stupidest thing you could do? Something that will ruin life as you know it?

I've got one now, standing at the butcher counter in King Kullen, the grocery store in the same strip mall as L.I. Lanes, the bowling alley cum billiard parlor I'm in the process of redecorating for its "Grand Opening."

I realize being in the wrong supermarket probably doesn't sound exactly dire to you, but you aren't the one buying your father a brisket at a store your mother will somehow know isn't Waldbaum's.

And then, June Bayer isn't your mother.

The woman behind the counter has agreed to go into the freezer to find a brisket for me, since there aren't any in the case. There are packages of pork tenderloin, piles of spare ribs and rolls of sausage, but no briskets.

Warning Number Two, right? I should be so out of here.

But no, I'm still in the same spot when she comes back out, brisketless, her face ashen. She opens her mouth as if she is going to scream, but only a gurgle comes out.

And then she pinballs out from behind the counter, knocking bottles of Peter Luger Steak Sauce to the floor on her way, now hitting the tower of cans at the end of the prepared foods aisle and sending them sprawling, now making her way down the aisle, careening from side to side as she goes.

Finally, from a distance, I hear her shout, "He's deeeeeeaaaad! Joey's deeeeeaaaad."

My first thought is *You should always trust your gut.*

My second thought is that now, somehow, my mother will know I was in King Kullen. For weeks I will have to hear "What did you expect?" as though whenever you go to King Kullen someone turns up dead. And if the detective investigating the case turns out to be Detective Drew Scoones…well, I'll never hear the end of that from her, either.

She still suspects I murdered the guy who was found dead on my doorstep last Halloween just to get Drew back into my life.

Several people head for the butcher's freezer and I position myself to block them. If there's one thing I've learned from finding people dead—and the guy on my doorstep wasn't the first one—it's that the police get very testy when you mess with their murder scenes.

"You can't go in there until the police get here," I say, stationing myself at the end of the butcher's counter and in front of the Employees Only door, acting as if I'm some sort of authority. "You'll contaminate the evidence if it turns out to be murder."

Shouts and chaos. You'd think I'd know better than to throw the word *murder* around. Cell phones are flipping open and tongues are wagging.

I amend my statement quickly. "Which, of course, it probably isn't. Murder, I mean. People die all the time, and it's not always in hospitals or their own beds, or…" I babble when I'm nervous, and the idea of someone dead on the other side of the freezer door makes me very nervous.

So does the idea of seeing Drew Scoones again. Drew and I have this on-again, off-again sort of thing…that I kind of turned off.

Who knew he'd take it so personally when he tried to get serious and I responded by saying we could talk about *us* tomorrow—and then caught a plane to my parents' condo in Boca the next day? In July. In the middle of a job.

For some crazy reason, he took that to mean that I was avoiding him and the subject of *us*.

That was three months ago. I haven't seen him since.

The manager, who identifies himself and points to his nameplate in case I don't believe him, says he has to go into *his cooler*. "Maybe Joey's not dead," he says. "Maybe he can be saved, and you're letting him die in there. Did you ever think of that?"

In fact, I hadn't. But I had thought that the murderer might try to go back in to make sure his tracks were covered, so I say that I will go in and check.

Which means that the manager and I couple up and go in together while everyone pushes against the doorway to peer in, erasing any chance of finding clean prints on that Employee Only door.

I expect to find carcasses of dead animals hanging from hooks, and maybe Joey hanging from one, too. I think it's going to be very creepy and I steel myself, only to find a rather benign series of shelves with large slabs of meat laid out carefully on them, along with boxes and boxes marked simply Chicken.

Nothing scary here, unless you count the body of a middle-aged man with graying hair sprawled faceup on the floor. His eyes are wide open and un-blinking. His shirt is stiff. His pants are stiff. His body is stiff. And his expression, you should forgive the pun—is frozen. Bill-the-manager crosses him-self and stands mute while I pronounce the guy dead in a sort of *happy now?* tone.

"We should not be in here," I say, and he nods his

head emphatically and helps me push people out of the doorway just in time to hear the police sirens and see the cop cars pull up outside the big store windows.

Bobbie Lyons, my partner in Teddi Bayer Interior Designs (and also my neighbor, my best friend and my private fashion police), and Mark, our carpenter (and my dogsitter, confidant, and ego booster), rush in from next door. They beat the cops by a half step and shout out my name. People point in my direction.

After all the publicity that followed the unfortunate incident during which I shot my ex-husband, Rio Gallo, and then the subsequent murder of my first client—which I solved, I might add—it seems like the whole world, or at least all of Long Island, knows who I am.

Mark asks if I'm all right. (Did I remember to mention that the man is drop-dead-gorgeous-but-a-decade-too-young-for-me-yet-too-old-for-my-daughter-thank-god?) I don't get a chance to answer him because the police are quickly closing in on the store manager and me.

"The woman—" I begin telling the police. Then I have to pause for the manager to fill in her name, which he does: *Fran*.

I continue. "Right. Fran. Fran went into the freezer to get a brisket. A moment later she came out and screamed that Joey was dead. So I'd say she was the one who discovered the body."

"And you are…?" the cop asks me. It comes out a bit like who do I *think* I am, rather than who am I really?

"An innocent bystander," Bobbie, hair perfect, makeup just right, says, carefully placing her body between the cop and me.

"And she was just leaving," Mark adds. They each take one of my arms.

Fran comes into the inner circle surrounding the cops. In case it isn't obvious from the hairnet and bloodstained white apron with Fran embroidered on it, I explain that she was the butcher who was going for the brisket. Mark and Bobbie take that as a signal that I've done my job and they can now get me out of there. They twist around, with me in the middle, as if we're a Rockettes line, until we are facing away from the butcher counter. They've managed to propel me a few steps toward the exit when disaster—in the form of a Mazda RX7 pulling up at the loading curb—strikes.

Mark's grip on my arm tightens like a vise. "Too late," he says.

Bobbie's expletive is unprintable. "Maybe there's a back door," she suggests, but Mark is right. It's too late.

I've laid my eyes on Detective Scoones. And while my gut is trying to warn me that my heart shouldn't go there, regions farther south are melting at just the sight of him.

"Walk," Bobbie orders me.

And I try to. Really.

Walk, I tell my feet. *Just put one foot in front of the other.*

I can do this because I know, in my heart of hearts, that if Drew Scoones was still interested in me, he'd have gotten in touch with me after I returned from Boca. And he didn't.

Since he's a detective, Drew doesn't have to wear one of those dark blue Nassau County Police uniforms. Instead, he's got on jeans, a tight-fitting T-shirt and a tweedy sports jacket. If you think that sounds good, you should see him. Chiseled features, cleft chin, brown hair that's naturally a little sandy in the front, a smile that…well, that doesn't matter. He isn't smiling now.

He walks up to me, tucks his sunglasses into his breast pocket and looks me over from head to toe.

"Well, if it isn't Miss Cut and Run," he says. "Aren't you supposed to be somewhere in Florida or something?" He looks at Mark accusingly, as if he was covering for me when he told Drew I was gone.

"Detective Scoones?" one of the uniforms says. "The stiff's in the cooler and the woman who found him is over there." He jerks his head in Fran's direction.

Drew continues to stare at me.

You know how when you were young, your mother always told you to wear clean underwear in case you were in an accident? And how, a little farther on, she told you not to go out in hair rollers because you never knew who you might see—or who might see you? And how now your best friend says she wouldn't be caught dead without makeup and suggests you shouldn't either?

Okay, today, *finally,* in my overalls and Converse sneakers, I get it.

I brush my hair out of my eyes. "Well, I'm back," I say. As if he hasn't known my exact whereabouts. The man is a detective, for heaven's sake. "Been back awhile."

Bobbie has watched the exchange and apparently decided she's given Drew all the time he deserves. "And we've got work to do, so…" she says, grabbing my arm and giving Drew a little two-fingered wave goodbye.

As I back up a foot or two, the store manager sees his chance and places himself in front of Drew, trying to get his attention. Maybe what makes Drew such a good detective is his ability to focus.

Only what he's focusing on is me.

"Phone broken? Carrier pigeon died?" he asks me, taking in Fran, the manager, the meat counter and that Employees Only door, all without taking his eyes off me.

Mark tries to break the spell. "We've got work to do there, you've got work to do here, Scoones," Mark says to him, gesturing toward next door. "So it's back to the alley for us."

Drew's lip twitches. "You working the alley now?" he says.

"If you'd like to follow me," Bill-the-manager, clearly exasperated, says to Drew—who doesn't respond. It's as if waiting for my answer is all he has to do.

So, fine. "You knew I was back," I say.

The man has known my whereabouts every hour of the day for as long as I've known him. And my mother's not the only one who won't buy that he "just happened" to answer this particular call. In fact, I'm willing to bet my children's lunch money that he's taken every call within ten miles of my home since the day I got back.

And now he's gotten lucky.

"*You* could have called *me*," I say.

"You're the one who said *tomorrow* for our talk and then flew the coop, chickie," he says. "I figured the ball was in your court."

"Detective?" the uniform says. "There's something you ought to see in here."

Drew gives me a look that amounts to *in or out?*

He could be talking about the investigation, or about our relationship.

Bobbie tries to steer me away. Mark's fists are balled. Drew waits me out, knowing I won't be able to resist what might be a murder investigation.

Finally he turns and heads for the cooler.

And, like a puppy dog, I follow.

Bobbie grabs the back of my shirt and pulls me to a halt.

"I'm just going to show him something," I say, yanking away.

"Yeah," Bobbie says, pointedly looking at the buttons on my blouse. The two at breast level have popped. "That's what I'm afraid of."

HARLEQUIN®

Super Romance®

*Looking for a romantic, emotional
and unforgettable escape?*

*You'll find it this month and every month
with a Harlequin Superromance!*

Rory Gorenzi has a sense of humor and a sense of
honor. She also happens to be good with children.

Seamus Lee, widower and father of four, needs
someone with exactly those traits.

They meet at the Colorado mountain school owned
by Rory's father, where she teaches skiing and
avalanche safety. But Seamus—and his children—
learn more from her than that....

Look for

GOOD WITH CHILDREN

by Margot Early,

*available August 2007, and these other
fantastic titles from Harlequin Superromance.*

LOVE, BY GEORGE *Debra Salonen* #1434
THE MAN FROM HER PAST *Anna Adams* #1435
NANNY MAKES THREE *Joan Kilby* #1437
MAYBE, BABY *Terry McLaughlin* #1438
THE FAMILY SOLUTION *Bobby Hutchinson* #1439

HSR71434

REQUEST YOUR FREE BOOKS!

2 FREE NOVELS PLUS 2 FREE GIFTS!

HARLEQUIN®
INTRIGUE®

Breathtaking Romantic Suspense

YES! Please send me 2 FREE Harlequin Intrigue® novels and my 2 FREE gifts. After receiving them, if I don't wish to receive any more books, I can return the shipping statement marked "cancel." If I don't cancel, I will receive 6 brand-new novels every month and be billed just $4.24 per book in the U.S., or $4.99 per book in Canada, plus 25¢ shipping and handling per book and applicable taxes, if any*. That's a savings of close to 15% off the cover price! I understand that accepting the 2 free books and gifts places me under no obligation to buy anything. I can always return a shipment and cancel at any time. Even if I never buy another book from Harlequin, the two free books and gifts are mine to keep forever.

182 HDN EEZ7   382 HDN EEZK

Name	(PLEASE PRINT)

Address	Apt. #

City	State/Prov.	Zip/Postal Code

Signature (if under 18, a parent or guardian must sign)

Mail to the **Harlequin Reader Service®**:
IN U.S.A.: P.O. Box 1867, Buffalo, NY 14240-1867
IN CANADA: P.O. Box 609, Fort Erie, Ontario L2A 5X3

Not valid to current Harlequin Intrigue subscribers.

Want to try two free books from another line?
Call 1-800-873-8635 or visit www.morefreebooks.com.

* Terms and prices subject to change without notice. NY residents add applicable sales tax. Canadian residents will be charged applicable provincial taxes and GST. This offer is limited to one order per household. All orders subject to approval. Credit or debit balances in a customer's account(s) may be offset by any other outstanding balance owed by or to the customer. Please allow 4 to 6 weeks for delivery.

Your Privacy: Harlequin is committed to protecting your privacy. Our Privacy Policy is available online at www.eHarlequin.com or upon request from the Reader Service. From time to time we make our lists of customers available to reputable firms who may have a product or service of interest to you. If you would prefer we not share your name and address, please check here. ☐

HI07

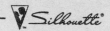

SPECIAL EDITION™

Look for

THE BILLIONAIRE NEXT DOOR

*by **Jessica Bird***

For Wall Street hotshot Sean O'Banyon, going home to south Boston brought back bad memories. But Lizzie Bond, his father's sweet, girl-next-door caretaker, was there to ease the pain. It was instant attraction—until Sean found out she was named sole heir, and wondered what her motives really were....

THE O'BANYON BROTHERS

On sale August 2007.

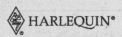

TEXAS LEGACIES: THE CARRIGANS

Get to the Heart of a Texas Family

WITH

THE RANCHER NEXT DOOR
by
Cathy Gillen Thacker

She'll Run The Ranch—And Her Life—Her Way!

On her alpaca ranch in Texas, Rebecca encounters
constant interference from Trevor McCabe, the
bossy rancher next door. Rebecca becomes very
friendly with Vince Owen, her other neighbor and
Trevor's archrival from college. Trevor's problem
is convincing Rebecca that he is on her side, and
aware of Vince's ulterior motives. But Trevor has
fallen for her in the process….

On sale July 2007

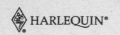

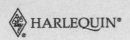